# Naked Jungle!

To Mike Garfin it looked like a simple
job to find out where Gerald Astley
was getting all his gambling money. But
suddenly it wasn't so simple, for young
Astley seemed to be involved in all the
degeneracy, perversion and sex-for-sale
activities in Montreal.

Astley's end was blackmail, and from
that comes sudden death. Sure enough,
he got his——and then the mob passed
the word that it was big Mike Garfin's turn!

---

"**Combines an unusual setting, characters
in the raw and the paradox of a highly
civilized city in the grip of Nature
at its most ferocious to produce a
strange, taut thriller.**

*Charlotte NEWS*

The first page of the 1954 Popular Library edition.

A NOVEL OF SUSPENSE

# HOT FREEZE

**Douglas Sanderson**

Author of *Blondes are My Trouble*

INTRODUCTION BY BRIAN BUSBY

A
Ricochet
Book

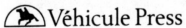

Véhicule Press

Published with the assistance of the Canada Council for the Arts,
the Canada Book Fund of the Department of Canadian Heritage,
and the Société de développement des entreprises culturelles
du Québec (SODEC).

Funded by the Government of Canada
Financé par le gouvernement du Canada | Canadä

Series editor: Brian Busby
Special assistance: Asa Boxer
Cover scan courtesy of Jim Fitzpatrick
Adaptation of original cover: J.W. Stewart
Typeset in Minion by Simon Garamond
Printed by Marquis Printing Inc.

LIBRARY AND ARCHIVES CANADA CATALOGUING IN PUBLICATION

Sanderson, Douglas, 1920-2002, author
Hot freeze / Douglas Sanderson ; introduction by
Brian Busby.

Originally published under the author's pseudonym of Martin
Brett : Toronto : Popular Library, 1954.
Issued in print and electronic formats.

ISBN 978-1-55065-400-4 (pbk.). – ISBN 978-1-55065-409-7 (epub)

I. Title.

PS8537.A63H6 2015    C813'.54    C2014-908340-8
C2014-908341-6

Published by Véhicule Press, Montréal, Québec, Canada
www.vehiculepress.com

Distribution in Canada by LitDistCo
www.litdistco.ca

Distributed in the U.S. by Independent Publishers Group
www.ipgbook.com

Printed in Canada on FSC certified paper

# INTRODUCTION

Brian Busby

THE MAN WHO WROTE this book wasn't a Montrealer, yet he captured the city better than almost anyone. He was born an Englishman, yet produced post-war Canada's greatest noir novel.

*Hot Freeze* is that work.

Martin Brett was Ronald Douglas Sanderson (1920-2002), a son of Kent, who came of age while serving in the RAF during the Second World War. Like so many thousands, after the conflict he left a devastated continent for a new life in the New World. Sanderson settled in Montreal, Canada's *ville ouverte*, where he found excitement and plenty of job opportunities: waiter, factory worker, jewelry store clerk, book critic, nightclub singer, actor, playwright, scriptwriter, and CBC radio host. He took on each, though it's as novelist that Sanderson is best remembered.

His debut was published in 1952 by New York's Dodd, Mead. The title, *Dark Passions Subdue*, was inspired by 'Yield Not to Temptation', an obscure 19th-century hymn by Horatio R. Palmer:

> Yield not to temptation, for yielding is sin;
> Each vict'ry will help you some other to win;
> Fight manfully onward, dark passions subdue;
> Look ever to Jesus, He'll carry you through.

Fight manfully onward…

A hardy, ham-fisted stab at serious literature, the novel is

5

nevertheless remarkable for its stark portrayal of homosexual desire set against the puritan backdrops of Westmount and McGill.

If the author is to be believed – and I see no reason why not – thriller writer 'Martin Brett' was born of a challenge from the same man who had inspired *Dark Passions Subdue*. The story goes that Sanderson was bet ten dollars that he couldn't write like Mickey Spillane.

Sanderson's second novel, *Exit in Green* (1953) – the first to use the Martin Brett *nom de plume* – is a stumbling, directionless murder mystery involving a down-on-his-luck playwright and a reclusive film star who dies in a tumble off a local landmark.

Or was she pushed?

Set in a fictitious town nestled in the Laurentians, the most remarkable thing about *Exit in Green* is that it was published not five months before *Hot Freeze*, Sanderson's finest work. It's with this third novel that the writer finds an uncommon voice that would serve as a meal ticket in the decade that followed.

*Hot Freeze* echoes something of Spillane in the way 'The Jean Genie' relates to 'I'm a man.' Both are integral parts of a continuum, all the while standing fully formed and defiantly apart.

For a time, I thought that it was the sex and the violence that made *Hot Freeze* the darkest of all Montreal noir novels. I now realize that the blackness stems from Sanderson's ability to create and maintain atmosphere:

> It was cold; bitterly paralysingly cold. There was
> a dampness in the air that bit into the marrow
> of your bones and stayed there. The red in the
> thermometer was below zero and still dropping
> steadily, and the weather forecasts offered no

immediate hope of a let up. The city lay rigid
under the stiffening blanket of snow. The air as
you breathed it felt solid.

And that is just the beginning.

Mike Garfin is perhaps the most Canadian of disgraces:
an RCMP officer who was kicked off the force. He risked
everything to sleep with a suspect's wife. He lost.

Sex.

Tessie, Garfin's girl, is a hooker. He'd marry her in a
flash, which isn't to say that he'd be faithful. No one is. Here
he's having sex with a young thing who minutes earlier wit-
nessed the murder of her lesbian lover.

Violence.

The body count in a Sanderson thriller is much higher
than any of his contemporaries.

Six months after *Hot Freeze* came *The Darker Traffic* (1954;
published in paperback as *Blondes are My Trouble*). A second Mike Garfin thriller, the dick is pressed up against a
prostitution ring operating out of a swanky downtown apartment building.

It's so very close to being as good.

Mike Garfin shouldn't be proud of much, but he can
claim title as the longest-lasting Canadian dick of the post-
war years. I write this recognizing that after *Hot Freeze* and
*The Darker Traffic* (I prefer *Blondes are My Trouble*) his history
becomes muddied. Nineteen-fifty-six saw publication of *The
Deadly Dames* , in which both character and creator take on
new names. For this outing, Sanderson adopts the *nom de
plume* 'Malcolm Douglas', while Garfin is recast as 'Bill Yates',
a private dick with plenty of trouble and a near-identical bio.

After a good break, our hero returns – as Garfin – in *A
Dum-Dum for the President* (1961), a Martin Brett thriller
with all requisite elements: willing women, corpses aplenty,

ridiculed rich and, more than ever, Sanderson's queer tangle of homophobia and repressed homosexuality.

*A Dum-Dum for the President* was published in 1961, less than a decade after *Dark Passions Subdue*. By that time, the bulk of Sanderson's writing lay in the past. He'd published seventeen novels in nine years, though only six would follow. The last, *A Dead Bullfighter*, appeared in 1975, more than a quarter-century before the author's death.

Sanderson's oeuvre totals twenty-three novels. Some were issued in hardcover, but most were paperback originals that came and went within a couple of months. A good number were translated into French. As *Mon cadavre au Canada* (1955), *Hot Freeze* found a home in Paris with Gallimard's *Series noir*. In 1975, it enjoyed an unexpected third life in German as *Heisser Schnee*. By that time, the English-language edition had been two decades out of print.

This edition of *Hot Freeze* – the one you hold in your hands – is the first in six decades. It also marks the first time a Douglas Sanderson novel has ever been published in Canada.

There should be more.

There will be more.

BRIAN BUSBY is Ricochet Books' series editor. He is the author of *A Gentleman of Pleasure: One Life of John Glassco, Poet, Memoirist and Pornographer* (2011), and is the editor of *The Heart Accepts It All: Selected Letters of John Glassco* (2013).

# 1

It was cold, bitterly cold. There was a dampness in the air that bit into the marrow of your bones and stayed there. The red in the thermometer was below zero and still dropping steadily, and the weather forecasts offered no immediate hope of a let up. The city lay rigid under the stiffening blanket of snow. The air as you breathed it felt solid.

Down in the darkening city the office workers, the store clerks, were finishing for the day; coming out of buildings to stand in clusters of frozen humanity waiting for the streetcars into which they would pack like cattle pressing one against another, trying to work up a sweat. Uncomfortable, sure, but a hell of a sight warmer.

All the same, it was good to be driving my own car this evening. The broken skid chain on the rear offside wheel was flaying my nerves by whacking the metal with every turn—but it was still good. The car was a maroon colored coupé, three months old and with its original shine, the sort of appearance that helps create an impression. I was on my way to the top of the mountain that stands in the center of the city, up where people have the money, and first impressions count for a lot. The guy who said that the higher up the mountain the greener grows the grass was thinking of Montreal: the greater the altitude the bigger the bankroll. And my potential client lived on Mornington Drive, right at the top. I needed any impression the car could make. A prosperous look and maybe I could jack up fees.

The house was a great graystone pile standing back off the road, three floors and a four car garage. I went up the shrub-lined driveway and parked right in front of the main windows where everyone could see the coupé if they looked out. I got out and ran over the squeaking snow to the front door, and the cold chewed like teeth at my ears, raised a numb bridge over the front of my nose. My eyes watered. I figured it must be at least twelve below. I just hoped a wind wouldn't rise.

I slipped into the foyer, closed the door quickly and rang the bell. The heat flowed around me and prickled my skin, making me feel good. That's the Canadian winter. Out in the street you nearly perish with cold. Step inside and you find the cold has made you feel you could kill giants. I rang the bell again. I was thawing fast and feeling good.

"Yes, sir?"

Butlers are scarce in Montreal, the local boys being averse to flunkeying. The maid who opened the inner door was a rawboned female of indistinct middle-age with the face of a beaver and a complexion like wild rose leaves scattered on snow. She called me sir. She didn't look as if she meant it.

"Mike Garfin," I said. "I have an appointment with Mrs. Remington for five-thirty."

"Bit late, aren't you? She's waiting." Whoever I hoped to impress, the maid was no longer one of them. She led me across a hall that wouldn't have looked out of place at Buckingham Palace: an oyster-grey carpet up to my ankles, a sweeping staircase over on the left, clusters of eye-tearing modern paintings hung all over the walls at pretended random, a cabinet of smokey wood filled with elegant and expensive-looking kick-knacks. The maid halted before a door and I mentally upped my fee by an extra five bucks a day.

"Your visitor, madame."

The intonation was smooth, perfect servant. You wouldn't have thought it was the same dame who answered the door. I stepped inside and on to a blue-flowered carpet a little thicker than the one before. Mrs. Remington was sitting on a settee, holding a glossy magazine. She put it down, rose and held out her hand as the door closed behind me.

I was surprised. I'd heard her voice on the phone, but I've been fooled by voices before. Mrs. Remington was one of those few women who look like they sound. Big, statuesque, supremely elegant. There are females born with the right to a sable coat and she was one of them. Reddish brown hair, blue eyes, long legs, a chest. She was beautiful, ripe and full like a rose on the day before the first petal falls. She looked about thirty-five. She was maybe forty. She wore only one ring, a huge star sapphire that slipped round and rubbed the center of my palm as we shook hands. I liked her.

"It's an awfully cold evening," she said in that voice of hers. "Would you care for something to drink?"

No, she wouldn't have anything herself. I poured a long one from a bottle marked Hennessy XO, planted myself in an opposite chair and waited for her to speak. She definitely did not like what she was going to have to say.

"Mr. Garfin, you're a private detective," she began, mustering.

"Inquiry agent," I said. "A question of licences. The local cops don't like having too many private detectives around town. They think it might be taken as a reflection on their own abilities."

"I see." She didn't, but it didn't matter. We sat and looked at each other while she mustered again. I didn't mind if she took her time. She was good to look at and getting better. It was long since I'd seen such a handsome woman, and not then with such class.

She picked up her magazine and began riffling her thumb along the edges. "Mr. Garfin, I know you will treat all I say with strictest confidence." She was embarrassed, not looking at me. "I want it kept secret. Even from my husband. I

13

asked you to call at this rather unbusinesslike hour because I knew he would be absent. He's going to New York by the five forty-five plane."

I guess the gleam in her eye was one of polite pride. She said: "You know of Mr. Remington, of course."

"Sure. Stockbroker, importer, art-collector, philanthropist, leading citizen, endower of hospitals—I even heard him once, giving an address to the local chamber of commerce. I was there by mistake. A good lecture. Very uplifting. But not sufficiently good to make me go running to him with stories of your private affairs. What do you want, Mrs. Remington?"

She hesitated, opening and shutting the magazine, looking at me as if debating whether or not I was worthy of trust. A lot of clients get like that, especially in the divorce cases I can't afford to refuse. I said: "I look like a treacherous rat, Mrs. Remington, but I'm faithful as a dog. Tight as a clam."

For the first time she relaxed smiling. "The contrary, Mr. Garfin. I expected you to be small and middle-aged and perhaps a little greasy, whereas you're young and large and—" She finished it with a feminine little gesture and leaned forward, opening up. "I'm worried about my son, Gerald. I'm afraid he's in trouble."

It was a flattening anti-climax. "Girls and babies?" I asked.

She shook her head, coloring faintly. "I almost wish it were. It might be simpler. No, Mr. Garfin, he's getting a lot of money from somewhere. He has a very liberal allowance, but not nearly so much as he spends. The other day he showed me more than eight hundred dollars."

"He has a cushy job you don't know about."

"No, he's only nineteen. He's still at McGill." She paused and the worry seeped down over her face like a bloom. "Gerald is somewhat headstrong. Five months ago he forged his stepfather's name to a check for five hundred dollars. I managed to cover it up, but I fear he's found a way of doing it again. He won't tell me anything. He laughs when I question him."

"Have you tried a good beating?" I asked. "You said stepfather."

"Yes, my husband and I have both been married before. Gerald is my first husband's child. You can see how really awkward the situation might become, can't you?"

She had laid down the magazine and was slowly, unconsciously, wringing her hands. "My husband is a man of very high principles and he and Gerald don't quite agree on certain matters—discipline and late hours and things like that. If he discovered that Gerald was getting money, well, dishonestly, there might be an open rift."

"A tough spot," I said. "And you want me to find out where the kid's getting the cash."

Behind me the door opened. Her eyes widened for a fraction: then she was calm, possessed, politely interested. "Yes, Mr. Garfin. And what do you think would be a nice color for the lampshades?" She rose to her feet, smiling at someone beyond me. "I thought you were on your way to New York, dear. This is Mr. Garfin. He's come to see about redecorating that hall."

I got up and turned round, nodding in response to the tiny bow that Remington made. If he were not a man, you might have said he was beautiful—much in the way that an object of his famed art collection was beautiful. He was tall and slim and wearing a conservative and perfectly tailored blue lounge suit. There was not a single unnecessary or spare angle to him. His thick hair was pure white, immaculately groomed. The few lines that enhanced his face had been put there by god and careful living. Behind his penetrating eyes was the look of utter serenity that comes with money and power. He was one of the richest men in the city. He was between fifty and sixty and as handsome as hell. Judging by the adoring expression on his wife's face, she would have married him had he been poor as a floating roomer. He looked at us apologetically.

"I'm going by the ten o'clock plane. At the last moment I learned that a shipment of pottery from Italy is waiting up at Halifax. I shall have to make some phone calls to arrange for a rapid transit." He turned to me with a polite smile. "How do you do, Mr. Garfin. You don't look at all like an interior decorator. Will you be able to make a good job of the hall?"

"Sure," I said. "Nothing to it."

"Excellent! Then I shall interrupt you no longer." He went out, walking like a man with well-knit muscles.

"Close," I said. "You think fast. Shall I leave now?"

She picked up the magazine and extracted a photograph from between the pages. "This is Gerald," she said, handing it to me. "The one on the left." I looked and saw two kids in their late teens, dressed in football togs and with their arms around each other's shoulders. They seemed much like any other kids. I tucked the picture into my inside pocket.

"I'll keep it. I'll follow him around for the next couple of days and maybe find a way of getting to know him. If he's discovered an easy road to the big money I want to be in on it." It was supposed to be a joke.

She didn't smile so I said: "My fee is thirty a day and expenses." She opened the magazine again, took out two fifty-dollar bills and handed them over in a nonchalant manner that made me wish I'd asked for forty. "Please accept this as a retainer," she said. "I'll phone you again the day after tomorrow. And thank you, Mr. Garfin; I feel less worried already."

We were halfway across the hall, making no more conversation, when the front door burst open and the two kids came in, stamping their feet from the cold. The boy I recognised immediately, except that I didn't know he would have flaming red hair and be higher than a kite—martinis, by the smell that approached with him. "Hello," he drawled and gave an airy wave, then he went straight across to a mirror and began combing his hair. Except for the deep voice, and maybe his shoulders, he was a pansy of the deepest lavender.

I thought I recognised the girl too, until I saw she was a young and female but nonetheless exact duplicate of Remington. Dark hair, grey eyes, the same look of self-discipline, the beauty intensified to a feminine and breath-taking degree, the same hard chastity—haughty as an iceberg and just as cold.

She flicked me a disinterested look from head to foot and murmured how did I do. I said I did fine and we went through the charade again of my being an interior decorator. Her name was Marian Remington and she was the result of her father's first marriage. Gerald's last name I learned was Astley, which made them stepbrother and stepsister.

And they sure acted like it. At least, she did. The cold, contemptuous glances she cast at his back would have frozen the pelt off an arctic seal. Gerald was still combing his hair and singing to himself—like the Lorelei. He was also watching me in the mirror. In the face of his stepsister's attitude his cheerfulness looked like wild insolence.

"I got word that Gerald was having a few pre-dinner cocktails at the Kipling," she said tartly. "I went to pick him up so he wouldn't catch cold on the way home. I hope you don't mind—Mother."

She said 'mother' the way the maid had called me sir; as a faintly derisive formality. Mrs. Remington smiled nervously. She seemed a little scared of her stepdaughter. I decided to get out, thinking it would be easy to pick up Gerald Astley at a later date, now that I'd met him. Too damned easy if appearance counted for anything.

Marian Remington was staring at me. "You don't look like a decorator. You're too large."

Her tone riled me. I said: "If I'd known you were going to

be disappointed I'd have cut myself down to your size." The boy turned briefly from the mirror to grin at her maliciously. He approved. She merely went stiffer.

"I didn't know you intended redecorating the hall, Mother," she said, with again too much emphasis on the last word. "Have you decided on a color?"

"Pink," I snapped.

"Are you being witty?"

There was a burst of amused laughter. "I hope he is, Marian dear. Pink would hardly be the ideal setting for these paintings." Remington was descending the stairs, dressed in a tartan dinner-jacket, looking the epitome of every cultivated host who ever moved through civilised society. The two women gazed up at him and, whatever their differences may have been, their expressions indicated at least one thing in common. Both of them idolised the man. Over by the mirror the kid stopped singing and put away his comb.

Remington advanced on us. I got a glimpse of the charm that had helped him make his high place in the community, and probably one or more of his millions. "A cocktail before dinner?" he said to me. "You are staying, of course." He saw me hesitate and added: "Of course you are. I've already told the servants."

From the corner of my eye I saw Mrs. Remington's face. I conjured up all I'd ever heard about painting, wallpaper and the disposition of color, and nodded an acceptance.

"I'll take you up on that drink, Pop," Gerald Astley said.

It was the last thing to call a man who looked like that, but the kid seemed to mean it. A trace of disappointment, almost sadness, flitted through Remington's eyes. "Yes, Gerald," he replied slowly. "Yes, but not too much or we will all spoil our appetites."

We drifted towards the room I had recently vacated. All except the girl, Marian, muttered something about changing her dress. I watched her disappearance up the staircase. She

18

was an annoying female. I watched the undulating retreat of her small backside and wondered if it had ever been slapped.

## 2

The dinner broke up a little before nine o'clock. I didn't enjoy it. The kid Gerald was looking at me with a calculating gleam in his eye, and it was a look I recognised. Only the thirty a day and expenses prevented me from putting him to rights, there and then. No one else was noticing what was going on. I anticipated minor troubles with him later in the evening.

The girl had little or nothing to say. She made a couple of attempts to get back to the color of the hall, but her father blocked her by saying I must be tired of talking business. After that she confined herself to projecting cold indifference at her stepmother and making only the odd, desultory remark. It suited me fine. She got even more beautiful when she was silent—more relaxed, somehow, and warmer. And with study her front view proved as provocative as her back. I was glad to be sitting opposite her. I considered reaching under the table with an accidental foot until I saw how her eyes hardened when they met mine. I was the first to look away.

With Mrs. Remington any sort of foot was out of the question. She was oblivious to everyone but her husband. Having got over her initial uneasiness at the situation she sat gazing on him and growing more radiant by the minute, sopping up his every word, bending on him a look such as mist men never see. Every so often she reached out and touched his hand, and despite the twenty or thirty years difference in our ages, I envied him. I envy any man who has a woman in that frame of mind. I looked around the table and wondered what civilisation was coming to. Dinner with two knockout females and the only person showing interest in me was a husky guy with red hair. Hell! Remington and I had discovered a common interest in salmon fishing. It carried us through the long meal. He talked knowledgeably and interestingly and I almost forgot that I was on a job. I had a feeling he could have talked just as authoritatively about all-in wrestling or butterflies or Ming pottery. And meanwhile his wife went on looking at him and the kid went on looking at me.

The job came back when I finished the last brandy and got up to go. Gerald Astley said he had a date, too, and maybe we could go together if I didn't mind giving him a lift. I had expected it. I said okay and made my farewells—a chilly look from Marian, warm politeness from her father, and an eager handshake from Mrs. Remington that indicated she hoped I would get to work right away. I didn't feel like it. The size and quality of the final brandy was making me drowsy. I wanted home and bed. We wrapped our scarves high and the maid let us out, wearing what looked like a knowing leer. We stepped outside and the icy cold woke me up with a bang.

"Hell!" Gerald Astley peered at the thermometer handing on the porch. "Nineteen below."

"Cool," I said.

"Oh, but we could soon warm it up if both of us really put our minds to it."

It was a sort of double remark. I ignored it, climbing into the coupé and turning up the heaters. He slid in beside me, sitting too close.

"Enjoy the dinner, Mr. Garfin?"

I never cheat a client. I had a job. I said: "The name's Mike. No, I was bored as hell."

It hit the mark. He patted my knee. We became pals. "Me too," he said. "Let's counteract it with a little excitement.

Two big guys like us could have a lot of fun together. I know some very nice interior decorators. What do you enjoy, Mike?"

"Almost everything. But maybe you and I wouldn't agree on the ultimate enjoyment."

"You never know," he murmured. "Sometimes it takes time. What do you suggest?"

"Your usual place first and my usual place afterwards, if we still feel like it. Where to?"

"Okay. Out on Decarie Boulevard and keep driving. This," he said, "is going to cost you money. Or me money. Or both of us."

The car turned out of the driveway, the rear chain still clacking. Gerald Astley began combing his hair again, humming a blithe little ditty.

I guessed where we were going. I kept my mouth shut. We drove for about fourteen miles over the snow-covered highway, on out to where the buildings thinned to nothing, out beyond the jurisdiction of the Montreal City Police.

The house was in a side lane, two miles off the main highway, well back behind a row of trees. It was a huge place, maybe a hundred years old, a type no longer built in Canada. Not a light gleamed from its windows. The vicinity was deserted. I drove over a rough track, past the trees and round the back. I had to search to find parking space among the hundred or more cars that stood there, headlights off. We got out and tracked to the front door.

This was a dive for barbotte, French-Canada's contribution to the world of dubious entertainment; the fastest, fairest, most panther-vicious dice game in the world, compared with which craps is a pastime for little boys and innocent maidens. Whoever runs a barbotte joint is an all-time winner. Overhead is at a minimum, a few tables with a fast-fingered banker at each. The customers bet against each other, covering each other's money on the Right Side or the Wrong

Side of the table, and taking it in turns to throw the dice. One Side wins, the other loses, depending on the throw. The dough being covered, dollar for dollar, no man can win more than even money and every man has a fifty-fifty chance. The banker stands by, says nothing, handles all the money, and collects five percent of all the table winnings for the house. Which sounds small until you remember that every table throws approximately once a minute. The medium sized houses take up to eighty thousand bucks a week. Only God and the graft takers know the rake-off of the bigger houses.

Barbotte is illegal. Once in a while the local Purity League investigates the racket and lodges a complaint with the Church. A church dignitary raps the knuckles of a politician who thumb-gooses the police department who immediately send out squad cars and arrest a lot of Friday-night bet-you-a-dollar men who are holding a penny ante barbotte session in a pal's basement. People are fined. The city sighs. Justice is vindicated and dignity upheld. The big boys continue doing a booming trade and graft takers buy another fur coat for the missus. And the population looks sideways and cynical at a majority of honest, overworked and underpaid cops who never get near the gravy and would probably spit in it if they did.

It's an exciting game. It can be a dangerous game. It's run by the Quebec Syndicate, the toughest crime outfit in the country.

"You're going to like this." Gerald Astley hit the door three times. I stood back in the shadows. The old doorkeeper and his wife had held this job for years. They knew me. A lot of people in this particular sphere knew me, and they didn't like me. A cop has to take orders from higher-ups. A private man, whatever his licence says, makes his own decisions. I'd managed to make myself unpopular in the past.

We went through the darkened foyer and into the gaming room. The light fell on my face and the doorkeeper recognised me, although he didn't bat a lid. Over in the corner behind a table his wife was dispensing soft drinks, alcohol not being sold in barbotte dives because a drunk French-Canadian is a tough hombre who won't lie down till he's dead. The doorkeeper's wife was selling Cokes at a buck a bottle. She was selling them till she saw me; then she stopped and slipped out from behind and disappeared. In a way I was relieved. The old biddie was painfully homely.

Gerald Astley had me by the arm, leading me to one of the big-time tables. His nostrils were flaring and I could see his top teeth. A gambler's look. It explained the need of the money. All I had to find out was the source of the supply.

"Don't talk to me," he said. "I want to get the lay."

I looked around. Besides the absence of alcohol there was an absence of women. Barbotte has none of the chichi polish that goes with roulette and chemmy, and when the smooth atmosphere is removed women are liable to act up. They don't like to see the money disappear so fast and so coarsely. They are usually lousy gamblers. They take up too much time. They are not welcome at barbotte games. Only a dozen of the two hundred or so players were females and they looked as hard as the males—who were something to see, some of them. Tough, soulless bastards representing every racket in the city; dead men, with the fast, wrenching throw of the dice as the only kick left to them; vicious sons of bitches, standing round the tables with money in their fists and life only in their glittering eyes.

Over at one of the smaller tables, I saw someone I knew, a little wiry guy with a pallid, pockmarked face and small dark eyes that darted like a snake's tongue. He came from Toronto where I'd first set up in business, and I'd not seen him before in Montreal. His name was Starkie and he hadn't noticed me yet. I turned back to the table and tried to be interested. Gambling for me is flatter than near-beer. The only diversion was a small American, talking wise with an Alabama accent and getting gypped by the banker who palmed a bill every time he passed the winnings. The American wouldn't thank me I told him. Neither would anyone else.

"I got it," the kid whispered, squeezing my arm. "The guy with the moustache playing Right Side is having a bad streak. I'll bet against him." He pulled out a cow-choker and covered the guy with a hundred-and-twenty. The banker's fingers fluttered like dragonfly wings.

"Aren't you playing?"

"Broke," I said.

The kid handed me a fifty. I planked and lost. "Enough," I said. "Take it easy."

"Plenty more," he said, breathing heavy. "Plenty-plenty more where that came from." I didn't ask him where. The kid was no dope, and anyway I was getting thirty a day and expenses.

But the moustache's bad streak turned to a good one. The kid dipped to another joe. The other joe began to win. In exactly fifty minutes the kid turned to me and he was flat. By my reckoning he had lost eight hundred and seventy bucks.

"Plenty more where that came from," I said.

"Sure. Wait a minute." He patted my shoulder and went across the room to a door at the back. I considered following and looked around. The doorkeeper was inside and watching me. His wife was watching me. A guy standing at the foot of the stairs with a hand in his bulging side-pocket was watching me. I went over to a small table and laid five dollars, trying to remember where I'd seen the gunman before.

The five bucks paid off. I built it to fifty, doubled it, and lost the lot. I threw another fin and lost again and that was enough. I quit. I turned around to leave the table, and there I was face to face with Starkie. He must have been watching me for a while. He'd had time to build up quite a fine fury for so small a man. His eyes were burning. He hissed a choice name at me.

"How are the brothers, Starkie pal?" I said, and I grinned. The Starkie boys used to be three, but now they are two. A couple of years ago the third member began stretching fifteen years behind the wall of Her Majesty's very private hotel in Kingston, Ontario. I'm proud of that achievement.

Starkie called me a couple of things, male and female. "Me and my brudder's gonna get you for that," he said softly. "We gonna ram that tin star where it'll make 'em bleed."

"Be a good boy," I said. "Go polish your pronunciation."

I walked back to the big table. Gerald Astley was waiting with a fistful of cash, looking at me with his tongue pressed against his upper teeth.

"Who's the pal?"

"Tried to bum a sawbuck. You seem to have had better luck."

He held the scrutiny a second longer, then settled down, grinning. "Credit's good," he said. "What I win I win. What I lose I don't lose." He was in a mood to talk, to brag. Two drinks right now of anything but Coke and he would jabber until his feet were touching his epiglottis. But there wasn't a chance of getting him away all the while he had dough in his hand. I stood and prayed he'd lose.

He did. This time I didn't count how much. When he turned away I offered him a cigarette and his hand was shaking so badly that he burned his finger on the lighter.

"Damn, I shall get a blister," he said. "What do we do now? I'm rationed to one good credit per evening."

"You're not such a big boy after all."

"Yeah? I can prove it."

Now he was putting double meanings into my mouth. "I know a couple of dames who'll suit us fine," I said coldly.

His eyebrows went up and suddenly he began to laugh. "Dear Mike, you said that with positive defiance. Did you think a woman would frighten me as I frighten you? Come, don't be so constrictedly old-fashioned. Something for everybody is my motto. Flesh, fur or feathers, I take them all. And they remember it."

"I'll telephone to see if they're occupied," I said. He followed me to the phone over in the corner of the room near the foot of the stairs, then excused himself to go to the washroom—to comb his hair, he said. I called Tessie.

Some guys have secretaries, so they can cry into their laps. Me, I have Tessie, a nice strapping Norwegian-looking blonde with too much meat for some but exactly my type. She listens to me when I'm low, lends me dough when I'm broke, and shacks up with me when the occasion arises, which is often. Once I asked her to marry me and she almost broke my jaw. Said I was insulting myself. They don't come any better than Tessie, whatever their profession. Through the earpiece she was calling me honey, wanting to know where I'd been the past five days.

"Busy?" I asked. "Someone with you?"

"I'll get shot of him. When you coming?"

"Half an hour. Get Marguerite. There's another guy with me."

"Cute?"

"I think he'd prefer a peg-house."

"Hell no!" she said. "Not one of them."

"Not strictly, he says. Claims to be all things to all people. Says he can teach everyone something. Brags a bit. He's nineteen."

"Nineteen!" Tessie let out a whoop of laughter. "Marguerite will scare the pants off him."

"Scare?" I said. "You're mixing your metaphors."

There was a gentle pressure on the lower part of my spine. A hand reached out slowly for the receiver hook.

"Bye, honey," I told her. "I have to see someone."

The pressure increased.

# 3

"Upstairs," a voice said. I looked over my shoulder. It was the gunman from the foot of the stairs and the hand was in his pocket but bulging more. He gave an extra prod. "The boss wants to see you," he said.

We made for the stairs like a vaudeville act, walking close together and in step. He looked like a touchy one; greying hair brushed with dye, and a lined face. Frightened eyes. The kind who gets scared and squeezes the trigger. I didn't argue. Up on the landing he pushed open a door and gave me a shove. The boss was waiting for me, a huge hulk sprawled in a swivel chair, finger tips pressed judiciously together.

I didn't know the other two in the room. One was a weazened bag of bones wearing a fedora some few sizes too big for him. He was twitching off the white mosquitoes—a panic-man badly in need of his powder. He made me jumpy. Addicts always do. He sat staring at me with everything moving but his eyes.

The other unknown was a fragile little blue-eyed blonde, about sixteen. A genuine mason's mate. She was sitting motionless, way back in a corner, looking as if she didn't know her nickel from her breakfast. She was pretty in the flaxy, womanless way those kids usually are, and my great bleeding heart wondered if I might do a little mission work to put her on the right path. Not at the moment, though. I was concentrating on the boss.

She was getting up slowly from behind the desk, stretching six feet of tweed-clad brown, a square hand rumpling the short hair, the wide features tightening. All her face needed was a good far cigar and a monocle. I was running the entire length of the daisy chain tonight.

I said: "As I live and breathe, Maisie Mackintosh. How long have you been running this joint?"

She flashed a quick look at her little blonde in the corner and I guessed we were in for some fancy showing-off. The infant's lips parted. The dull look almost left her china eyes. Maisie came round the desk at me, heaving her stevedore shoulders. The gunman patted me over, put my gun on the desk and covered me from the front, holding his gun like a professional and too far for a swift poke.

"Okay," Maisie grated. "Start talking." The little blonde shivered with the delicious toughness of it all.

"About what?"

She spat out a mouthful of really creamy profanity. "I said talk. What are you snooping after?"

"Maisie, language," I said. "In front of the chid, too."

The little guy stopped twitching and tilted back his sombrero for a better look. "I don't like this smart bastard," he said in a thin whine. "Let's fix him."

"Shut your mouth, Charlie. I'm doing the talking."

Maisie was giving it to us out of the side of her mouth. It would have been funny if I didn't know Maisie so well. She was not a funny woman.

The guy with the gun was still giving me the frightened eyes. I tried to remember where I'd seen him before. I wondered what Starkie had to do with all this, and thought that if I kept quiet they might be forced to put some information into their questions.

Maisie was wearing the original great stone face. "All right. What goes with you and the red-haired fairy?"

"Maisie," I said. "Curb this morbid curiosity for the abnormal. Confine it to the home front. Tell you what I'll do." I nodded at the infant in the corner. "I'm bunker-shy, so if you'll let me take her then you can have the youth, red hair and all. In fact, I think your establishment just purchased him for you. You won't get much out of him, but I'll guarantee baby here will get plenty out of me."

She called me a bastard.

I didn't like it. I got mad. "Wrap it up," I said.

She balled her fist and lunged. I feinted and smacked her hard across the face with the back of my hand. She went back against the desk and put out her hands to steady herself. Her face was dead white except for the mark on her cheek. She was insane at being made a fool of in front of the girl.

"Okay," she said, not moving. "Give it to him."

Frightened-eyes was moving closer. The little twitches stood up and flicked his sleeve and I saw the flash of a bone-handled knife. I looked down to see if the gun had a silencer. When I looked up the eyes were more frightened yet and I remembered at the same moment he did. It was the hair-dye that had been fooling me.

"Hello, Killigan," I said. "How are things in Manitoba?"

He stopped dead, gulping. His lips moved two or three times before any sound came out. "Damn it, Maisie, I know this guy. He's a Mountie. I ain't fixing no goddamned Mounties."

"You stupid whoreson," Maisie spat out. "Fix him. He's a phoney would-be copper from Montreal. He's been getting in people's hair for the last two years, and now he's getting in mine."

"Sure I am," I said. "The RCMP moves in a mysterious way. Like God. Tell her how I sent your partner up the river, Killigan."

"It's true," he said doggedly. "His name's Garfin. I ain't fixing no bloody Mounties. The whole mucking pack would be down on my ears."

"Wise boy." His gun at the moment was about as lethal as a stick of peppermint rock. Maisie was wavering. The only danger was from the twitcher, still holding his knife until his knuckles showed. I had to take a chance before he got nervous. I picked my gun from the desk and tucked it into my pocket.

"Sorry I couldn't stay, Maisie. Some other time." I turned

to the useless looking little blonde who was huddling deeper into the corner. "And some other time for you, eh sweetheart?" I clicked my tongue at her.

Maisie hissed a sweet name at me.

"Your dirty mouth gets monotonous, honey," I said. "I ought to knock you in it once more just for luck. 'Bye now."

I walked out of the room, feeling easier when the door was between me and the knife. I went downstairs taking my time. It would be hours, maybe days, before they could check up on the truth. The Royal Canadian Mounted Police are not notoriously eager to give out information, especially about a man who has been kicked out of the Force.

It was getting on for midnight. The red-haired kid was nowhere to be seen. I went into the washroom to see if he'd found some other pal; then I went into the gaming room to wait. Starkie was still at the small table. I went to the large table and watched. I was in no mood for any sort of small talk.

Another half hour and the kid still hadn't shown. I trailed over to the back room to see if he was in making another touch, and found myself face to face with a far baldheaded man I'd never seen before who jumped when I went in and let his hand hover around an open drawer. He was alone so I came out again and over to the phone to call Tessie, who was impatient and wanted to know where the hell we were. The kid wasn't there, either. I said to give my apologies to Marguerite and we wouldn't be down. Tessie started to rant and then softened, asking in a worried voice if I was in trouble again. I told her to forget it, go to bed, and I hung up. The Royal Canadian Mounted Police had once grafted me on a conscience and it was beginning to bother me. I was getting thirty a day and expenses and not earning it. I went through the front door where the wife was pinchhitting for her husband, and out into the dark. The cold burnt into my lungs, wrapping around me like an iron shroud. The line of trees looked ready to snap in the brittle air. I dug my hands deep, hunched my shoulders, and went round to the back.

A dim figure was stooped by the bonnet of the coupé. I spoke to him in French. I knew he had no English. I said: "Fixing me a time-bomb?"

The doorkeeper straightened up. "A nice car you have, Monsieur Garfin, my friend. I thought your headlights were shining. Please, you will not switch them on until you reach the main road."

"You mean this place is secret?" I said. "Haw! Now push!"

I got in and drove down the rough track with the skid-chain clacking and flacking like a riveting shop. The cold white countryside rolled by me on either side. The chill had got into the car. I shivered.

I reached the highway and turned toward the lights of Montreal, endeavouring to get myself into a brighter mood. I had a vague idea. I tried to cheer up by pretending it was a solid hunch.

# 4

It was two hours before the vigil paid off. I was parked near the top of Mornington Drive and facing downwards, all my lights off, about twenty yards from the entrance of the drive to the Remington house. I couldn't withdraw any farther and still see because the snow had started to fall in a curtain of little white beads. I had to screw up my eyes and peer through it, grateful for the dim light of the street lamp about the same distance away on the other side of the entrance. The cold seemed to have diminished. It always does when the snow starts falling. But I still had my heaters on, and I was getting sleepy.

I almost missed the guy when he arrived. A few late

homecomers had passed me during the wait and I thought he was another of them. He passed under the light, hands in his pockets, hat pulled down, collar up. He looked like anyone else. His silhouette was vaguely familiar, but it wasn't Gerald Astley. Too short. He turned into the entrance of the Remington drive.

I gave him a minute's start, to catch him at whatever he was doing. Then I slipped out of the car, through the gates and silently up the snow-blanketed driveway.

It wouldn't be the windows. The double-windows would be on for the winter, both locked up against snow and cold. I tried the front door and found it locked. I went along the side, past the garage and round to the back of the house. The storm door was standing ajar. The inner one was unfastened. I eased inside, knowing by the smells that I was in the kitchen. I stood perfectly still and listened to nothing but the dripping of a tap. I pulled a pencil flashlight from my pocket and checked my gun in the shoulder holster.

The layout of the house was confusing to me. I had entered before by the front door and now I had trouble figuring where I was. It was a big house. I floundered through two more rooms and opened several doors before I got to the hall. I crept to the stairs and realised I must be leaving a trail of wet footprints on the oyster-grey carpet. I flashed the light behind me and there wasn't a matching set of marks. Maybe the guy had gone up the backstairs.

I reached the upper landing and searched again. The carpet was a sapphire blue and even my own prints were no longer showing. There were no lights. Another flight of stairs led up to the third floor. I started to climb. A thin gleam showed under a door directly facing the top stair. A low murmur came faintly to me. I heel-and-toed the last few feet and pressed my ear to the door, listening. I couldn't catch a word. I hefted the gun into my right hand, silently opened the door and stepped in.

The girl was sitting with her back to me, on a low stool in front of a dressing table. She was singing to herself. She stopped when she saw me, not bothering to turn round, looking at me via the reflection in the mirror, smiling, her eyes gone wide like ox-eyed daisies. "Oh, good!" she said with a little giggle. "You've come to attack me, haven't you?"

She was dressed in an unbuttoned fur coat and nothing else. She had legs that went up to her hips, and the smooth hard-looking thighs of a tiger. Even in the dim light I could see that her eyes were a dark yellow and dizzy-looking. I didn't need to ask who she was. Her resemblance to Gerald Astley was pronounced. I guessed she was younger than her brother.

"What's your name?" I asked.

"Geraldine," she said. "Geraldine Astley. My, but you're a lovely thing."

Her voice sounded as dizzy as her eyes. She giggled again. I said: "Button your coat and show me where your brother's room is."

She didn't move. She gave me a long, languorous smile. "A friend showed me a photograph tonight where the girl was dressed exactly like this. I was practicing. Look." She put her foot on the stool so that her knee was almost touching her chin. The coat swung right open, disclosing a profiled buttock. "Am I attractive?" she asked. "To you, I mean? Would you like a photograph of me?"

"You're swell," I snapped.

She waved an arm. "I could show you some pictures of you'd like. I have heaps of them here."

I was beginning to suffer. I grabbed the fur-clad shoulder and jerked her to her feet. "You're brother's room," I said. "Quick and quiet."

"Oh, all right, you mean pig." She pouted. Suddenly her voice made me think of the smoke from a wood fire. A smell was coming from her, subtle and faint and feminine.

She opened the door and led me down the first flight of stairs, moving like an over-lubricated Blue Persian kitten. My palms were greasing with a film of sweat. I was hoping I could be wiser tonight than in the past.

She closed the bedroom door behind us before switching on the lights. "I knew he wouldn't be here," she said sulkily. "Why are you so interested in Gerald?"

The bed was a smooth expanse of unrumpled silk. The room had an untouched feeling. Whoever had been here knew exactly what he was looking for and had taken it without disturbing anything else. And if it was blackmail, the evidence was removed. Probably the guy was back in the street by now, being picked up at a corner by a fast car. I swore under my breath.

"Why are you so interested in my brother?"

I stopped scanning the room and looked down at her. I looked too long, and suddenly the lessons of past experience got themselves good and lost. Perhaps it showed in my face. She knew the exact moment when the last scruple was gone beyond recall. The fur coat slipped back until her arms were half out and I could see the smooth expanse of her bare shoulders. She moved close until she was standing only an inch away from me. She said: "You're having a hard time aren't you?" The coat slipped right off as she stood on tip-toe and wrapped her arms around my neck, fastening her teeth gently onto my lower lip, balancing herself so that only her breast was touching my jacket.

There was something wrong with her. One half of my mind went sick—disgusted—but it was too late. The furnace was lit, the steel was forged with the pounding blows of a steam hammer. I locked with her, pulling her flat against me, pushing my mouth down on her soft wet lips until her neck was bending. She drew back, breathing rapidly, then lowered one of her arms and put a hand on me.

"My God!" she panted. "Oh, my God."

There are lessons that a guy like me doesn't learn until he's too old to need them anymore. I picked her up and thrust her squirming body down on her brother's unrumpled silken bed.

It was not until later that I realized the lights had been left on. She lay with her head on my chest, her hands still on me, giggling something about Shakespeare having been wrong when he said you needed darkness. She was having a fine time. "What's your name?" she asked.

"The hell with my name," I said, and I was angry. She was suddenly talking to me as if I were a small boy, a not very intelligent spaniel. I didn't like it. She moved her head and looked at me and I saw that she was really regarding me as just an accessory. I liked that even less. It grated on my pride. It dug at the roots of what I fondly consider to be my manhood.

Her hands were moving possessively. She murmured something I didn't catch about a poet named Garcia Lorca. Then she quoted two lines of poetry. They almost crisped my ears. I pulled away and got off the bed, and she was holding her arms out to me. "Quit," I said. "I'm leaving."

The look in her eyes changed completely. She jerked out something pretty raw and her teeth gritted together.

I said: "Put your coat on. You might take a chill."

Her eyes were soft and completely evil. "Again," she said, "or I can invent a plausible story and get some attention by screaming."

I wondered whether to clout her. There was no need. Someone chose that moment to tap on the door.

This, I realized was a classic situation. The thought was no comfort to me. The girl lay there quite still, smiling, watching me zip and button, not moving even when the tapping was repeated. A woman's voice said softly:

"Are you there, Gerald?"

I opened the door about a foot, blocking the view. Mrs. Remington was outside on the landing, dressed in a négligée

35

and holding a hot water-bottle in a woollen cover. "Oh, it's you Mr. Garfin." She looked at me blankly. "It's a cold night and I thought Gerald might need this." She held the bottle out to me.

"He's not here. I'm waiting for him."

"Oh." Her features appeared to melt and then remould into a mask of worry. It occurred to me that I'd never seen such a magnificent looking female before. She was majestic. She said: "Is he all right? I thought I heard voices."

"You did, Mama," the girl behind me tinkled brightly. "It was your little Geraldine." She jerked open the door and stood beside me, casually buttoning the fur coat and scratching the back of her leg with a bare foot. "This wonderful man was roaming about the house looking for Gerald's room. I volunteered to act as a guide."

Mrs. Remington turned to a pillar of ice, but she stayed polite, became even more so. "Mr. Garfin, this is my daughter Geraldine. Gerald's sister."

"But, Mama, we've met," the girl said, revving up an idiotic laugh.

I said: "There is a perfectly reasonable explanation to this, Mrs. Remington."

"I'm sure there is." Her attitude was betraying nothing. I wondered what I'd do in her position, with two such ungovernable little bastards for children. She said: "Perhaps you would like to leave now, Mr. Garfin, by the way you came. And, if you can, as quietly."

"Sure, Mrs. Remington. I'll phone tomorrow to check something about Gerald. To check something with Gerald."

"Please do," she said. "I shall expect it. Goodnight, Mr. Garfin."

Out in the streets the snow had lessened, a wind was rising, blowing up from across the frozen river. Tessie would have worried about me had she known, been afraid that I'd catch cold. A nice girl, Tessie. Jealous, but nice. All at once I had the familiar need of her that has beset me in the most unexpected places since first we met.

But I had a greater need to hit the hay. I drove down from the mountain, carefully, through the rutted and crackling snow, and turned out toward the suburb of Notre Dame de Grace—Our Lady of Grace. I was still thinking about the girl. Like brother, it seemed, like sister. It was no wonder that no one had mentioned her at dinner that evening. The family might not realise what Gerald was, but with little Geraldine it was obvious. It would have proved difficult to keep some indication of the knowledge out of the conversation if she had been made a table topic. It wouldn't surprise me if they had some unspoken agreement not to mention her name when she wasn't around. I wondered what the austere looking Mr. Remington thought of his growing step-daughter. Not that I was sorry for him. He had compensation, and more, in his wife.

I determined to do a little devious lying to her when I called the house tomorrow, to steer the conversation so that it cleared any suspicions she might be entertaining as to why I took so long to answer the door when she knocked. But maybe she had no suspicions. After all, she had told me 'please do' when I said I'd be calling. I switched on the dashboard light and looked at my reflection in the side window. Maybe I didn't look the type that went around violating young girls. Or even being violated by them. Maybe the thirty a day and expenses were safe for a little longer. Maybe. Nuts.

I parked the car in front of the duplex, because it doesn't have a garage. If the temperature dropped to more than thirty below even the anti-freeze would freeze, but that's a normal hazard of Canadian winter motoring. The cold chawed at my knuckles as I took off a glove to get my key. I guessed the thermometer was reading about twenty below and hoped it would go no lower. I opened the front door, stepped into the small entrance, and kicked over the milk bottles, which I do unfailingly every night.

There was no cause for alarm. The flat is a narrow oblong in shape, and when Miss Lindsay rented me the front two rooms she moved her bed to a small room right at the back beyond the kitchen where few sounds penetrate. There was no question of self-preservation or guarding her virtue in this putting of distances between us. Miss Lindsay has few illusions about anyone, but she is seventy-two years old and considers herself beyond the reach of masculine wiles. She also has an accent, and although she came from Scotland fifty-nine years ago she sounds as if she got off the boat yesterday. It makes her hard to understand when she gets excited, a fairly frequent occurrence since she reads nothing but ghost stories and the more gory murders. It was now only three o'clock in the morning so she was probably sitting up in bed with a book in one hand and the other automatically stroking her large and docile ex-tom cat, which she calls Sir Walter Scott. I set up the milk bottles, closed the inner door and entered my bedroom.

Someone had been at the whisky. There were two glasses on the bureau—only one of them used—and the remains of a forty-ounce bottle that had been full when I left the house. There was also a muffled snore. I turned and saw a guy asleep in my bed, on his side, with his back to me, the covers pulled over his head so that only a tuft of hair was showing. It wasn't Gerald Astley. This hair was dark. The guy looked to be big by his outline—as big as, if not bigger than, myself.

I went back out and down the passage to see if Miss Lindsay had left me any coffee. She had. The light was on in her room. I knocked.

"Who is it?"

I opened the door. "Who do you think it is, you old rake? Look. Entertain your boy friends on the sly if you like, but keep them in your own bed. I pay good money for that room."

Miss Lindsay, a God-fearing Presbyterian who neither smokes nor drinks, and says 'brother' only in moments of stress, gave a shriek of laughter that sent Sir Walter Scott leaping to the floor. "Och, you're a circus," she said. "And that poor laddie waiting for you all night with only me for company."

"So when it got late you let him have my bed. We'll give his address to the Salvation Army. They can send up a few more."

"Don't fuss. I made you a bed on the settee in your sitting room."

"The hell with the settee," I said.

Miss Lindsay enjoys herself when I snarl at her. She was bubbling like a tea kettle. "Now, you know you wouldn't have me drive his sweet little face out into the cold to look for some nasty damp hotel. And him enough like you to be your brother."

"Like me?"

"Aye, poor lad."

"Yes," I said. "You probably did right."

I went back along the passage and into my room. I lifted my foot and gave the figure a kick on the bump of its backside. "Wake up," I said loud. "The day of glory has arrived."

He stirred and groaned and rolled over, bringing his face from under the blankets like a rising hippopotamus.

The Lindsay was a mile wrong when she claimed that Tom Littlejohn's was a sweet little face. Not even his mother would have said that. But it was sure a good face to see after more than four years. I grinned at him.

"Where you been?" he growled.

"Out."

"I know that, you stupid moose," he snarled. "Get and break open another of those bottles of liquor before I get and break you open. And move. Quick."

He got out of bed with the speed of a tiger and lunged at me. I hit him back.

# 5

So we drank whisky and called each other bum and louse and occasionally punched each other around a little. We finished the second bottle of Seagram's VO and switched to some Queen Anne, and I knew I was earning myself a princely hangover. Tom Littlejohn didn't have to worry. I've seen him take another bottle when almost everyone else has been under the table for an hour. And get up clear-eyed and bouncy the following morning. He hadn't altered.

I first ran into Tom at training depot, back in the days when I was fragrant enough to think the Law was a fine thing that everyone should be forced to obey. I was even willing to do some of the enforcing myself. He was in the same entry and the trouble started because we were supposed to look alike and some people couldn't tell us apart. Me—I didn't see it at all. We were the same size and color, but the resemblance ended there. He was straight Scot and looked it. I was Irish-French and looked neither. Both of us disliked the continual mistake in identity, and consequently each other.

When Tom discovered that the name Mike concealed the French version 'Michel,' he took to calling me Meeshell, with perfect pronunciation but making it sound as if it came from a sneering water-faucet. The payoff came one evening when he called me Mee-shell after I'd been mistakenly bawled out for something he had done. I suggested that his face be altered to prevent the mistake occurring again. He said it was a swell idea, and we went to the gym. When we finished we were even less distinguishable than before, having beaten each other's faces to a uniform pulp, and there was nothing to do but bow to the inevitable. We went out and got drunk together, taking another guy with us. The other guy's name was Danny Menzies, and eventually the three of us got to be known by the corny title of The Three Musketeers. Danny Menzies was a good head. Everyone liked him.

At a much later date it was Tom who stood up for me when I was deep in trouble through having gone to bed with a wife when I should have been apprehending her husband. I was wrong and deserved no support—deserved worse than actually I got. Of all uniformed forces, the Royal Canadian Mounted Police is the hardest to join and the easiest to leave. I was permitted to resign.

It was just as well. I'm not the stuff of which Mounties are made. Anyway, the pay is bad, so looking at it from a sensible angle I'm better off. At least, that's what I tell myself when I think about it, which is seldom. And they're better off without me. Every ten days they get enough applications to fill the enlistment needs for a year. They can select guys with more enthusiasm, more singleness of purpose than I've got. Guys who can look at a bed and a babe without wanting to put the two together.

But I always remained grateful to Tom. Once I wrote him a letter and told him I was broke and he sent me three hundred bucks by return of post. It enabled me to set up in business in Toronto. I still owed it to him.

We finished the Queen Anne.

"Come to collect your dough?" I asked.

"Among other things. Mind if I stick around a couple of days? Mary Queen of Scots and her cat seem to think it'll be okay."

"She's lavish with my bed. Sure, it's yours. I can bunk on the settee. You on leave?"

He emptied his glass and poured another. "Did I tell you I'm a sergeant now?"

"Congratulations. So you're not on leave. Anything I can do to help?"

He sat chewing his underlip. "Purely for interest—what do you know about the local narcotics set-up?"

"Two or three pushers and a handful of bindles. A couple of dives. Nothing about the big boys who run the trolley, unless you can feed me a lead. That's why they made you a sergeant, huh?"

"They've sent me in plain clothes. Keep it to yourself. I'm not known in Montreal. We've pretty well closed off the Pacific traffic in Vancouver, but there's a big pipe opened here in the East. Something new. Mercks from Germany, Italian morphine, number one grade Spanish cocaine—the works. Some of the boys think it's brought in by the immigrants. I've checked and rechecked. The supply is too regular and the marketing methods better organized than anything in history. Immigrants, hooey! I think I got a lead."

"That's what I asked you," I said.

"Right! We'll start in a couple of days. First I want to take a rest. You working on anything?"

"At the moment I'm not sure."

"Hell, not another dame." He saw me grin and said: "You ought to operate on yourself. Don't you ever learn? Be like me and wait till you get a couple of days off. Like now, for instance. Where can a man who's pressed for time pass a lazy afternoon?"

"Marguerite," I said. "She shares a place with a friend of mine named Tessie."

He wanted to know so we discussed her. Then he went on to tell me of the female delinquent he had tried to reform, out among the snows of Northern Alberta. It was a funny story, but he didn't fool me. He was thinking of something else—wondering, I guess, whether he was going to pull off his first solo assignment and justify those shiny new stripes recently given to him. The Mounties are all the same, every damn one of them; always worrying about whether they're going to prove themselves worthy, always sticking at it until

42

they do. I sat and listened to Tom and got drunk and talked until the morning came creeping a bluish-grey over the piled snow outside. Then I fell asleep. When I awoke again it was eleven o'clock and I had a ferocious head. Tom must have put me to bed.

I took a shower, felt better and went to the kitchen to find him sitting over late breakfast with the Lindsay. She was alternately having minor hysterics and gazing at him raptly while he sang Will Ye Gang tae the Highlands, Lizzie Lindsay, in a burlesque Scotch accent. You couldn't have moved her from the table with a team of Clydesdales. Had she known he was a Mounted Policeman she probably would have swooned with sheer delight. It was nice to see them getting on. I liked them both.

I said: "And now he's been wooing you some more, I suppose you'll delicately suggest that I move to the cellar so that he can have both the rooms to himself."

"He's aye bitching," Tom told her. "Take no notice. Wait till he hears I want to borrow his car and a topcoat."

"Poor Tommie," Miss Lindsay lamented. "He has just the flimsiest rag and it's twenty-two below outside."

"Poor Tommie," I said. "He can have my raccoon."

"Not me. You don't catch me in no fur coat in the city. It's okay for you slick Easterners, but—"

"I have only one other," I said. "The tweed I wore yesterday."

"I'll take it."

Miss Lindsay murmured approval. I could see where Sir Walter Scott and I were going to have to move over a piece. The cat was watching Tom with a scowl.

"And the car?"

"Pick it up later, at my office on St. Catherine East."

The Lindsay objected that it was a long way for the poor lad to come in the cold. I stood my ground. I was also shudderingly firm about not eating a huge breakfast of fried bacon and kidneys. My mouth tasted like a U-boat commander's sock after he had been at sea for some months. I sluiced down three cups of scalding coffee and left them. They had resumed their community singing.

It certainly was twenty-two below outside, with every little degree making its icy point, but I didn't like wearing the fur coat either, there being a space between the ages of twenty-two and forty-eight when such things are not permissible. Particularly did I object to this coat. It was a gift from a grateful client, a well-heeled female of advancing years who was known around town as the Youth's Companion. During the two weeks she employed me to trace an alleged nephew—he turned out to be a deserter to greener pastures—she switched her loyalty from Youths to Private Detectives. The raccoon coat had been the ultimate weapon in her last violent assault. I didn't want it. She told me not to be silly. Then after listening to my speech entitled 'Take back your gold, for money cannot buy me,' she turned so poisonous that I changed my mind and decided I'd earned the coat in extra fees. Nevertheless, and despite the row, if she saw me wearing it around town she would probably come galloping like a springbok—and that sort of money I don't want. She has a face that will someday make a fine door-knocker on the gates of Hell.

Hell! This day was a white one. During my spell in the Mounted I spent a time up north in the Barren Lands, where the blizzards go lashing for weeks on end. But the Barrens are a paradise compared with Montreal when a biting wind makes every pedestrian keep his head down, and the traffic takes every corner on a swooping arc of ninety degrees. What with last night's whisky and the prevailing conditions, I arrived at the office feeling I'd just toured the seven circles of the Inferno.

The greasy stairs to the second floor above the grocery store looked seedier than ever. The streetcar bells outside were making an especially noisy noise. I tottered up with assistance from the bannister and wondered if there was anything left in the bottle in my safe. I opened the outer door and Mr. Remington was sitting in the ante-room, reading *Fortune* and looking out of place.

He stood up with a polite smile. He was groomed, healthy, imperturbable and immaculate, a fine example of the clean life I wasn't leading. He said: "You keep late hours, Mr. Garfin."

"Yes, I had to go and model for this coat."

He stood around as I unlocked the inner door, followed me in, and waited patiently until I indicated the only other chair with my finger. He sat down, not adjusting the knees of his pants as I'd suspected he would. He looked at me with a graveness that in no way disguised the fact that this morning he was addressing someone slightly inferior to him. I decided to leave the bottle in the safe for a while.

"I thought you were in New York," I said.

"I blame you entirely. Your conversation last night was so interesting that by the time my phone calls were made I had missed the plane."

"I don't believe it," I said, "but it's pleasant. What do you want?"

He took out a gold cigarette case, offered me one, snapped it shut and replaced it in his pocket. "Mr. Garfin," he said, "I progressed from a half a million to three millions purely by calling people 'sir.' It made business a pleasure for everyone. Not least of all, for me."

"I'm unambitious," I said. "Also, I understand that in those cases the first half million is the toughest."

"Quite. You can never make it by deception."

"Now if I were the Chamber of Commerce I might believe that."

"You're far too nervous for a Chamber of Commerce."

"You're damn right. I've just driven through a few miles of Montreal traffic."

He paused, drawing deep on his cigarette. He wasn't being nearly so nice as last night. Polite yes, but not nice. It showed in the set of his mouth, the way he scrutinised me as if I were a rare but unsavoury bug. I wondered what little Geraldine had eaten for breakfast, and if it had made her talkative. I said:

"I can offer you a drink, but nothing else unless you tell me what you want. What is it? Your study redecorated? New curtains? A change in the position of the chandelier?"

Then he smiled, knocking forty years off his age, and I knew little Geraldine had still been asleep when he left the house. "It was a ridiculous pose," he said. "You make a very poor decorator. But I gather you to be an excellent fisherman, which is possibly better."

"Yes, that was okay. I enjoyed it." I got up and took the quarter bottle from the safe. One of the glasses was gubby so I gave him the cleaner one. He nodded my health and drank off half. I said: "What's the trouble?"

He smiled again, laying down the drink on the desk. "I'm going to let you into a family secret, Mr. Garfin. My wife and I share a complete confidence with each other. Either one of us is constitutionally incapable of withholding anything from the other. This morning she came to me and told me that she had hired a private detective, and that the private detective was you. She also wanted to tell me *why* she had hired him, but I forbade it. It was a refinement of our confidence, Mr. Garfin. Even the momentary wish to withhold something gives her the right to continue doing so until the matter no longer troubles her, which undoubtedly it does at the moment. My wife loves me, Mr. Garfin. To share her trouble with me would only be to double it for her."

"She's a nice woman," I said.

"I could see last night that you thought so. It made me extremely proud. When one admires something it is gratifying to see the admiration reflected in others."

The guy was batty about her, and who could blame him. I said: "So what do you want?"

He drew out a quality wallet that must have cost a slice of its contents. He extracted two crisp one-hundred-dollar bills and laid them on the desk without a flourish. "Please believe me," he said, "that this is in no way a reflection on you. You appear to me to be an honorable young man and I'm sure my wife is of the same opinion. But her conscience is bothering her. She feels that in hiring you she has abridged our treasured mutual confidence. The result is that she no longer feels a need of your services." He nodded delicately at the money. "Will you accept this sum as a termination of your employment?"

"I certainly will," I said.

The wallet was still out. He was riffling his thumb over the remainder of the wad. "And would you," he asked, "accept another two hundred in return for telling me why my wife employed you?"

"Ah, Mr. Remington, now that's a simple question of ethics. You can go to hell. And if you offer to raise the figure I shall have to kick you downstairs."

"Indeed?" He extracted another century and added it to the the two on the desk. "Admirable! Splendid! Mr. Garfin, we shall go fishing together when the season begins. I have a house up in Gaspé." He got up, tucking away the wallet, buttoning his coat, giving me full benefit of the straight-forward gaze. "You know, you may yet make that first half-million. It is possible that in the future I may be in a position to offer you a few uninteresting but fairly remunerative tasks. Call me from time to time."

I picked up the three hundred bucks. "Thank you, sir. Good day."

He walked to the door, smiling to himself, turning when his hand was on the doorknob. "And now that we've concluded our business so amiably, young man, may I ask you for a frank opinion of my stepson, Gerald?"

"You may," I said. "He needs a swift kick with a hobnailed boot."

Remington gave an enormous and unexpected guffaw. "Quite. Quite so. Very succinct. Perhaps one day I shall employ you to take him in hand." He shook his head, still laughing. "No, no, don't say anything. I'm merely guessing. I have no wish to make you even inadvertently break that code of ethics you mentioned. Good day."

I sat admiring the incomparable beauty of the hundred-dollar bills until his footsteps had faded down the stairs and merged into the clanger of St. Catherine Street. Then I picked up the phone and dialled.

"Mrs. Remington," I said, pitching my voice high and refined.

It was the beaver-faced maid who had answered the door. She was also using her high-class intonation. "Whom shall I say is speaking?"

"Just bring her to the phone. It's a surprise."

"To everyone but you, chum," she snapped. "When you call this place you give your name."

"Okay, you recognise me and win a cigar. Now fetch her."

"She's out."

"Then get the gilded youth."

"Male or female?"

"Male. What's the difference when you're gonna give me the same answer?"

"That's right," she said sweetly. "He's out."

"Me too, I expect."

"Absolutely correct. But you're right out." She hung up.

I opened the drawer of my desk and took out pencils, rubber bands, erasers, paper fasteners, pen nibs, string and thumb tacks. These are known as office supplies. When first I opened my office I thought I'd need them. I bought them in bulk.

I didn't need them. I've seldom handled more than one case at a time and I don't keep permanent files, having no wish to tempt burglars and, as yet, no desire to take up blackmail when I get too old to work. So I was stuck with the office supplies. They got in my way and annoyed me, until I figured a method of getting rid of them.

I make animals. It is very soothing. This morning I started with a giraffe, which is easy. I stuck a pencil into an eraser, unbent some paper fasteners for the legs, fastened on a string tail with a thumb tack, and used a small eraser for the head. I even achieved a reasonable pair of ears. It was a pretty good giraffe. When I was satisfied I pulled it to pieces and threw as many of the office supplies as were damaged into the wastebasket. My second animal was less recognisable but more interesting.

Whenever some dewy-eyed damsel tells me how exciting it must be, being a private investigator, I try to compute just how many soothing animals I have constructed in my time. The figure is astronomical. If anyone is thinking of adopting the profession and the concomitant game, I recommend try making a recognisably lifelike rhinoceros. It takes longest and is the most soothing beast of all. But whatever animal you pick, there'll come a stage when you've soothed yourself almost to a point of madness. On good days it takes up to three hours. Today I managed it in fifty-three minutes.

I picked up the phone and arranged my larynx to resemble Charles Laughton's.

"Are you there?" I said. "Might I speak to Mrs. Remington, please?"

"Good," the maid said. "Very, very good. Can you do Cary Grant?" She hung up.

I prayed that as she turned from the phone she would break one of the valuable ornaments and be fired on the spot.

More animals were out of the question. The bottle was there, but I drink only for dog-hair purposes, and after sundown. The only other offices in the building, a fur salesman and a lead-pipe wholesaler, were at lunch and wouldn't have talked to me if I wanted it, which I didn't. There was nothing else to do. I put the bottle away, stuck on my hat, locked the office, and went across the road for coffee and a smoked meat sandwich.

It was cold all right. I bought a newspaper which said in jovial tones that this was the longest cold spell since nineteen-something-or-other, that it would continue, and that it would get even colder. On the same page were pictures of people skiing in the Laurentians, only forty miles away. This made me sour. After which I read Walter Winchell's column and got sourer. By the time I finished lunch, sitting at a counter stool with the elbow of the person on either side rammed into my rib-cage, I was fit to be tied. I gave a couple of jabs of my own—for reprisal purposes—and went out without leaving a tip, feeling I'd been pushed around. I decided to take a turn at a little pushing myself. It would be especially nice to go up to Mornington Drive and push the beaver-faced maid.

The car was parked in a side street, directly alongside the office. I crossed the street, dodging the antiquated street-cars, and scrunched over the snow to where the coupé was waiting. I got in, inserted the ignition key, turned it and started up. The windows were heavily frosted and I didn't see anyone coming. I put my hands on the wheel and on either side of me the doors opened simultaneously, freezing my knees with a crossing wind. My hands stayed on the wheel. Without turning my head I could see the guns held tight, almost invisibly, against their hips. Then the doors closed and I had company, was snuggled between a nice warm body on either side. The one on my left had taken the wheel. The one on my right was pressing his gun into the side of my belly. I sighed deeply and said, "Hello, boys."

The Starkie brothers had caught up with me. They were regarding me with an unholy relish. They didn't resemble each other much except for the flickering eyes, shining with sweet anticipation. The one I had seen at barbotte was holding the gun. The one at the wheel ripped open my overcoat, dipped in and took my gun from its shoulder holster, dropping it into his pocket.

He studied me intently. "I was up to Kingston Jail the other day to see my brother Brian," he said roguishly. "He sent you back a little present."

I didn't say anything. I've learned not to. We sat in silence for thirty seconds while the sweat formed on my back and ran in a little trickle down my spine.

"Now whadya think a that," he exclaimed in injured tones. "All that trouble to bring a gift from dear old Ontario, and what I get? No thanks at all. Nothing. But do I mind? Me? Nah! I deliver it anyway."

He closed his hand and cracked me across the face with a force that snapped my neck back and started a singing in my ears. The breath came whistling through my nostrils. I said nothing.

"There," he said happily. "I'm thoughtful, ain't I?"

"Not far to go, Joe," his brother said. "Lotsa time. Let's get moving."

"With pleasure. With a great deal of pleasure." Joe backed the car slowly into St. Catherine, ground the gears and turned east, grinning like a death's head. My death's head. I tried to swallow the lump of fear in my throat. It wouldn't go down.

# 6

It wasn't far. The trip took less than five minutes. We pulled up once, to allow a mob of passengers to surge into the road and board a streetcar. I beamed frantic thoughts, trying to will one of them to turn and look through the windshield. They kept their heads down against the wind, rushing for the open door like lemmings. We drove on.

We pulled up, still on St. Catherine Street East, about three-quarters of a mile from my office. Joe took his hands off the wheel and covered me again with a gun, smiling the while. His brother opened the nearside door a fraction, looked both ways along the sidewalk and suddenly said "Clear." Joe gave me a shove. It was beautifully arranged—formal, like a minuet. The boys were experts.

I cursed my luck that the sidewalk in this part of town is only five feet wide. One second my feet were on it. The next and I was halfway up a steep and narrow flight of stairs. I had time to see only the neon sign that hung above the entrance. The Romilly Club. Prop. Jean Genet. The Starkie brothers were hustling behind me in a lethal little nubbin.

"Get rid of the car, Joe."

"Yes, Henry."

The feet pattered off downstairs and Henry stuck the gun more forcibly into my back. Somewhere upstairs an orchestra played about sixteen bars of music and stopped again. The club band was having an afternoon rehearsal.

I didn't take a chance and make a run towards the music. The third Starkie brother, whose name was Brian, once killed the bother of a client of mine in cold blood. He got fifteen years. Henry Starkie's blood was of exactly the same temperature, and he would get off with nothing at all. He'd be back down the stairs, round the corner, and set up with a cast-iron alibi before the police arrived.

"Keep moving," he said softly, and I did just as he told me. The band started playing again—a calypso. Through a slightly open door on the second floor I saw them on the orchestra stand, wearing the faintly green expression that night club workers wear of an afternoon. I guess it was nothing compared to what I was wearing. Henry moved faster, and so did I. The gun was skewering my back and Henry was breathing too hard for anyone's comfort. We went up the next flight of stairs to the third floor like a pair of whippets. Something like this had happened last night and I reflected on how monotonous it could get after the first time. Downstairs a guy began singing, and the band went really loud as always in a calypso vocal. They sounded cheerful. I could scream my head off up here and no one would know the difference.

But whoever made me scream, it wasn't to be the Starkie boys. Sure, they might do the punching, the twisting, the burning—maybe even the killing—but they'd be simply the instruments. There was someone else behind this, someone with influence enough and money to use the top room of this club as a chamber. The place looked plush. The Starkie brothers had never had more than six bits between them— two bits apiece, and too much at that. And they were the sort of hoodlums who couldn't influence themselves a streetcar ticket. I tried to think of my other enemies. They were plenty. A thin film of sweat covered my face.

I thought the door on the landing had opened of its own accord. Starkie gave me a sharp push and a foot came out so that I tripped and went sprawling. When I picked myself up and turned around the other guy still had his hand on the doorknob where he'd been listening for our approach. He closed the door and smiled.

It's bad enough when a guy is vicious. When he's big at the same time I don't like it. This one looked as if his idea of a joke would be to tear the legs off a new-born baby. He was also as big as a coal truck. I'm a fair size myself. He topped me by about five inches and a hundred pounds. The fear-lump in my throat grew to the size of Gibraltar. I said:

"Okay, what's it all about?"

"You're gonna find out right soon, pal," the big boy answered with a delivery he obviously thought was richly funny. "Won't you kindly have a seat?"

I sat down on a chair, looking around me. The room had a window and one other door and looked like the sitting room of an apartment. Etchings on the wall, a small cream settee, a black and white color scheme. Downstairs the band was beating hell out of the percussion section.

The big boy clicked his tongue. "No, no, no, pal. Not like that." His elegant patience appealed to Henry who stood in a corner, still holding the gun, passing his tongue over his upper lip and giggling. "We want you to sit the other way, pal. Like you was riding a horse. With your chin on the back of the chair. And with your coat and jacket off."

"How would you like to go for a wee-wee on a high-powered cable?" I said.

It wasn't right. He was not amused. I saw his ham fists open and close and wondered why he didn't sock me, why he didn't move. The door opened and Joe Starkie slipped in, his mean little features gathered up with eagerness.

"How's it go?"

"Our pal is just gonna take off his coat and jacket."

I did what the man said. There was no choice. I sat astride the chair like I was just riding the Queen's Plate winner down the stretch.

It was the big guy who tied me with my throat pulled down against the top of the chair, my back curved like a dromedary's hump. A very professional job, but gentler than I expected. I wondered why.

Henry put away his gun. "Let me at him." He was almost pleading.

"Lay off," the big guy growled. "No marks. You know what the boss said. We got trouble enough as it is." He tied a final knot and stood up. "We're ready now, ain't we pal. Someone call Lofty."

I could raise my eyes enough to see part of the room. Joe Starkie was standing by the window, eagerness in his jittering eyes. The big guy sat on the cream settee, his big feet wiping rhythmically over the fur coat I'd dropped on the floor. Henry went over and knocked on the inner door. We're ready now, Lofty," he called. The door opened.

Henry Starkie was runt enough, but the guy who stood there was shorter by a foot. I thought at first he was kneeling; then he moved forward and I saw that four-feet-five was all he would ever be. It was not the result of an accident. He had been born with feet in about the position where everyone else has knees. It looked especially bad on him because his shoulders were as broad as he was long.

He was tough—one of the mild, systematic tough ones, with too much self-confidence. He was, to put it mildly, homely. His arms were thick and he had enormous hands. In the middle of his face was the biggest nose I've seen on anyone, hanging down over a large mouthful of jagged teeth and a nutcracker jaw. He was holding a length of rubber piping, and by the way he swung it I knew it was weighted. I knew what was coming and would have been sick if my throat hadn't closed over.

Henry stood in front of the chair, looking at me longingly. "Aw, let me at the guy for just two minutes."

"No marks," the big guy said.

"This won't mark." Henry laid his hand on my head and jerked out a fistful of hair. He laughed excitedly. I made a resolve that if I ever got out of it I'd pluck his little scalp hair by hair, with a hot needle.

The dwarf they called Lofty gave Henry a gentle push that sent him flying beyond my range of vision. "Stay away," he ordered in a low, soft voice. "This is my job." He put a thick finger under my chin and lifted my head until I was looking into his dog's eyes. "What's new, Mr. Garfin?"

"Nothing." I was having difficulty with a dry tongue. "Some-one has miscued, bringing me here. I've never seen the place before, or any of you except the Starkies. Maybe they've made an intentional mistake to work off an old grudge. Don't get involved."

"They don't  have that many brains between them." He tickled my chin with the finger, smiling a wistful smile.

"What's new, Mr. Garfin?"

"Nothing," I said. "Nothing at all."

Slowly, with a regretful sigh, he moved to the side where I couldn't see him. The rubber pipe hissed through the air and hit my curved back, just above the kidneys. It didn't hurt. It hissed again and landed in precisely the same spot, and I could stand it. It came down a third time and the pain went jangling round a livid framework that started somewhere in my heels and ended in a tight area of unendurable agony in the back of my head. Then, when I couldn't stand anything else, he hit me again—a fourth time—and I thought I was going to spew blood. "Okay," I gasped. "What is new? What do you want to know?"

"That's better." He came to the front, trailing a huge and soothing hand over my back and shoulders. "That's a nice body you have there, Garfin. Well-developed muscles.

"I'd like to use them on you sometime."

"A natural reaction." He studied me, head on one side like some grotesque bird. "You're something of a gentleman, Garfin. Most times if I commend anyone on their appearance, especially when I'm persuading them about something, they come back with some dirty crack about their also having nice long legs. You didn't do it and I like that. You're a nice fellow." He paused, nodding approvingly. "Now what was it you wanted to tell me?"

"What do you want to know?"

He wagged his finger under my nose. "Come now, you lead a hectic life. You must be full of new things. The new client you got yesterday for instance. All the new information given to you by the young man with red hair. You must have found it so exciting that you immediately passed it on to various friends of yours. Who did you tell, Garfin. Tell me."

"I know nothing," I said. "You're crazy. The only client I got yesterday wanted me to trace a missing necklace."

"Tell you what. I'll pass the time while you think it over."

He went beyond my line of vision again and the other three moved their heads forward very slightly. Then the pipe started coming down with slow regularity, always on the same fifty-cent sized spot, and after a while I couldn't see anything at all. The tracery of shrieking pain was extended now, right to the tips of my fingers, up into my eyeballs, not missing a half-inch. The orchestra downstairs went soft and suddenly swelled to five thousand pieces, and a woman began to sing in a high piercing wail at the end of a long dark alley. Then it wasn't a woman any more. Something went wrong with the echoes. I was listening to a choir of demented angels singing from a long way off, singing down a ringing length of sewer pipe. The voices rose and fell and rose and fell and then they merged and went back to a single note. All at once I realised I was listening to myself howling. I passed out.

I was slumped with my Adam's apple pressed against the back of the chair. My eyes were closed. I was trying to pick something out of the blur of voices. One of the Starkie brothers was complaining that it would take all day and the big guy mumbled something about there not being any marks. I couldn't make out what came after because a solid black wave wrapped itself around my head. When I came out again the Starkie boys were still beefing, and one of them was suggesting that they do it now. The tone of his voice told me that 'it' meant the end of me, and I didn't care. I was relieved. I was tired of life and the cold weather and working for a living. I was tired, above all, of having my kidneys beaten to a pulp. Then very distinctly the dwarf said:

"We have to find out first if he told anyone."

"There wasn't anything to tell," I said. "What do I have to do to convince you guys?" I opened my eyes. They had changed positions. It was Henry now who stood at the window. He smiled lovingly at me and turned his back. The others gathered in.

"But we heard different," the dwarf said with a practice

flourish of the rubber. "We heard you leaned a lot last night. What was it? And who did you tell?"

"For the last time," I began. I stopped. Henry had whirled from the window and seized brother Joe by the collar, shaking him like a rattle. He looked panicky. "You crazy bastard," he shouted. "You stupid goddam ox. Where didya leave his car?"

"In the side-street," Joe protested, knocking the arm away. "We gotta take him off in it, ain't we? Whatsa matter with you. No one ain't gonna find it."

"No? Take a look. There's a guy leaning against it looking like he's gonna stay."

They crowded to the window, except Lofty who could barely reach the sill. His lips were drawn back, disclosing most of his unattractive teeth. He said: "What's happening?"

The big boy turned round. "There's a guy opened the door and got in the front seat."

"Maybe he's gonna drive away," Joe suggested hopefully.

"He's gonna stay."

The dwarf came forward and the swinging pipe hit Joe square in the face. He went down into a corner with the blood gushing from his nose. It was a cheering sight. "Very careless, Joe," the little one said; then he turned to me. "Who is it?"

I said: "I guess he followed us. Maybe he thinks this is a social call. In a little while he'll get suspicious and come on up. We Mounties always work in pairs."

The pause was brief, but utterly silent.

"You goddam liar," Henry snarled and drew back his fist. The dwarf stepped between us.

"It won't work, Garfin. You tried that last night, so we knew in advance. You've been a private investigator a couple of years in Montreal and before that for two years in Toronto. That's where you met the Starkie boys. You sent one of them to jail. You gave evidence in court, under oath. You didn't mention then that you were a Mountie."

"Sure not," I said.

"The Mounted Police don't leave a man on undercover work for four years—if you can call a private eye being under cover."

"You figure it out," I said. "We're pretty shrewd boys."

"Wait," the big guy said, looking into the street. "I think he's driving away."

My heart plummeted to my boots, nearly taking me with it. I offered up a prayer and wondered what had become of my stomach.

"No, he's looking at his watch. He's looking around. He's looking up here."

"Sure he is," I said. "He'll be here himself in a few seconds."

"You liar!" the dwarf was crumbling fast. "Why did you let me beat you up?"

"They train us that way. I might have learned something."

"Liar!"

"You silly sawn-off little bastard," I snapped, riding it hard to convince him. "If you were big enough to see over the sill you could check for yourself. He's six-two, dark hair, my build and wearing a thick double-breasted herring-bone tweed coat."

"That's right," the big guy said nervously.

"He's still lying."

"Sure. We'll sit around and wait till he comes up. It's all the same to me."

Joe got up from the corner, mopping his nose. The little guy found himself the center of attraction. The three of them were waiting for him to do something, to make a decision one way or the other. I sweated another gallon, hoping something would happen before Tom got fed up with waiting and took the car.

"Well?" I asked.

The dwarf gritted his mal-occluded teeth together, making tiny snapping noises. Then his glance darted twice towards the door from which he had first emerged and I said: "Maybe you'd better go in and consult the boss. Better still, bring him out here. There's not a lot of time."

He swung the rubber piping and gave me a furious lash on my back. I bit the insides of my cheeks and waited for the nausea to pass. "Temper," I admonished. "Get your boss."

The door opened slowly and the boss walked in. He was medium-sized with a fat shiny face like a cheese and a paunch that came almost to a point. His thin hair was slicked down and his currant eyes were as wide as they could get, which wasn't very. He wore a suit that must have cost two hundred bucks and on him it looked like two cents. He was French-Canadian, and his pudgy, purple-colored little hands were raised shoulder high in horror.

"What 'appening 'ere?" he gasped, looking fearfully from one to the other. "Why you 'ave that man tied up?"

"Your act is as lousy as your English," I told him in French. "Tell your boys to get these ropes off. Quick!"

He wasn't the same man when he spoke his own language, not nearly so cute. He stayed oily, but a hard core appeared—like a well-greased nail. He said: "I do not like liars, Monsieur Garfin. Are not you and your friend afraid of being arrested for false pretenses?"

The big guy at the window said: "He's out of the car and walking up the sidewalk. He's looking in a store window."

"Just a couple of minutes more," I said. I knew it wasn't true. Tom was tired of waiting and about to beat it. I wondered if he had yet reported to headquarters and took my chance. I hated to do it, but there was no choice. I said: "His name's Tom Littlejohn. He arrived last night from Alberta to help me on an assignment. He's a sergeant. Check with local headquarters. Say you've got some information for him. Ask if he's in the city yet."

Pointed-belly went out of the room and I heard the click of a phone dial. He murmured something I couldn't catch. Within a minute he was back, eyes wide again. "Untie him," he said in English. He switched to French. "There's been a mistake, monsieur. A bad mistake. Someone told us many lies about you. How can you forgive us?" He cleared his throat, sliding a hand toward his pocket. "A little gift? A compensation, monsieur? Two hundred dollars? Three hundred dollars?"

"Stuff it!" I snapped. "I don't forgive that easy. You'll be hearing from the boys."

His face hardened. "I run an honest business here, Monsieur Mountie. I cannot help it if you come here for a drink and go away with wild stories about being tied up. You have no witnesses. You have no bruises. I shall make a great deal of trouble if the Mounted Police began to persecute me. I am an honest citizen."

"Yeah," I said. The ropes were off and I stood up. A screeching pain went two ways from the middle of my back and clamped my waist. I put on my coat and jacket, moving fast lest Tom should disappear.

But had there been an oncoming tidal wave, I should have waited for one thing. I walked across the room and took the piping from the little guy's hand and threw it into a corner. Nobody moved. I grabbed a handful of his hair and lifted him until he was on tip-toe. I said: "I don't like you, little one," and then I slammed him real hard, right on top of his massive nose, releasing his hair so that he sank gently to the ground in an untidy little heap.

It was lovely. I looked at the others. "I'll work up to you bigger sizes later on," I said, and went out leaving them motionless behind me. I scuttered down the stairs as fast as my aching back would allow. The music was still coming from the second floor.

They had looked scared. People had really been that scared of me once, when I had the Force behind me. "The

61

Mounties will get you." No idle threat that—except when I made it. The Mounties wouldn't get anybody for my sake. For my sake I doubted they'd even cross the road. And if I talked myself blue in the face they probably wouldn't believe me. Not that I blamed them. The odor left behind when I resigned was a powerful one. It was only natural that they'd looked the other way and held their noses ever since. Except Tom.

I hit the sidewalk like a ruptured rocket. He was ten feet away, looking into a window full of topcoats. I went up behind him and touched his shoulder. He saw my reflection in the glass.

"Got to get myself a new one," he said. "Can't keep wearing yours. Hell, but it's cold!" He turned around, took a look and grabbed my arm. "You're pale green, sonny. I warned you before about canned lobster."

"My back," I said. "There are no bruises. Put your head close and keep talking. Also keep walking. They're watching from an upstairs window."

"Do I go up and pay them a visit? It's months since I had any proper exercise. Tell me the particular one you especially don't like."

"None of them," I said. "There's nothing you can do. No witnesses. You'd be a constable again within a month. Let's get to the car."

"Nothing I can do?"

"Nothing at all."

He opened the front door of the coupé and eased inside. He got behind the wheel, lit a cigarette and stared at me hard. "By crack! I can remember a time when—"

"So can I," I said. He was looking disgusted at me and it hurt. So what could I do? Nothing. My thirty a day and expenses were still covered, which meant I still had a client until fired by the client herself. A rule.

"Back to the office," I said.

Tom let in the clutch and we slid along St. Catherine

Street. The wind was blowing fiercer. Little eddies of snow were lifting from the sidewalk.

# 7

He poured the last of the whisky onto my back, rubbed it in, tucked my shirt away and put the empty bottle back into the safe. I picked myself up off the desk, feeling better, although I hated to see good whisky put to such a use.

"So what else?" he asked.

"Nothing else. I figure the kid is blackmailing someone. Being a fairy, his scope for blackmail is probably fairly extensive. And being a fairy, he's probably very talkative, especially to his close friends. Last night he was giving me the eyes out at the barbotte joint. Somebody put two and two together and made six."

"You mean they are systematically beating up all his pals?"

"Okay, so it's a lousy theory. How's this? He tried last night to milk whoever it is of a second wad of dough. They wouldn't pay off. He started threatening. They said he wouldn't dare make public whatever he knew. He said he had already, by telling me. Now they want to know if I have told anyone else."

"A little better. Not much. How about this Mrs. Remington?"

"I think not. She wouldn't have called me in the first place if she had any deep dark secrets."

"Women," Tom said with a grin, "can be pretty mysterious." It reminded me of what I'd said the night before about the Mounties. There was something I had to tell him. I said:

"In the past twenty-four hours I've got out of two tight spots by pretending I was still with the RCMP. This afternoon I had to give extra proof. I told them your name and who you were. It'll be all over town within an hour."

For a long time he looked at me incredulously, without moving, and then he began to curse. Tom is not a very good curser. He was repeating himself within a couple of minutes. I might have laughed, had he not been so deathly serious. He gave a final repetitive explosion, scratched his head, shrugged his shoulders and stood with his arms dangling at his sides, looking helpless. "Well, that jiggers that," he said. "I'll take a couple of days holiday and report back."

"I'm sorry," I said. "I'm sorry, Tom."

"Sure." He grinned. "Why not quit for the day? Let's go."

"Not for me. I still have some unfinished business. You push off and have a good time on your own. Visit Marguerite. And take the car. I'll not be needing it."

"Sure," he said. "Sure." He stood a while longer. "Don't feel bad, son. It's only a question of replacing me. They won't know the next guy." He waved a hand. "See you soon, then."

Yes, they'd replace him. His brand-new stripes wouldn't be affected. But when would he get another assignment like this? Next year? Ten years? I figured I stood fair to have loused up his career. At best to have put a crimp in it. A sergeant in the army is damn all. In the RCMP he's big stuff. Proud. Every commissioned officer is selected from the ranks, usually from the sergeants. I sat and thought about it and was anything but proud. But hell, I couldn't let them take me for a long cold ride. No more than I could help feeling lousy at what I'd done.

I picked up the phone and got the City Police. I asked for Captain Masson.

Some three hundred and fifty years ago the tough, hard-headed bunch of Normans who were Masson's ancestors came to Canada with the intention of establishing another France in the New World. They didn't make it. The British came along and took the country away from them. But in the main those ancestors didn't fail. Masson carries on the tradition by being French Canadian and Quebec to the last pore of his skin. Besides which, he is so transparently honest that I sometimes wonder how he reached the rank of captain.

"What do you want?" he growled.

"I saw a sign this afternoon in St. Catherine East. Romilly Club. Prop. Jean Genet. What do you know about this prop? Short, fat, oily, paunchy. Uses his hands."

He made a long, thinking sound. "Genet. Yes. Ran a book. Blue Bonnets race track and ice hockey. Small rackets. Made most of his money selling drink to the Indians out at Caughnawaga when it was still illegal. Got caught once and did three months. Opened the Romilly about a year ago. Going straight, so far as we know. Why?"

"Idle curiosity," I said. "Thanks. Incidentally, somebody's swiped my gun. Don't fall for any obvious murders."

His voice went several notes deeper. "You getting into more trouble, Garfin? Some of the boys down here are only waiting for that slip."

"And your boss, Mr. Frankisson?"

"And my boss, Mr. Frankisson, especially."

"Bless his stony heart," I said. "And because I speak French doesn't mean that my name is pronounced Garfann. It's Irish. Gar-finn!"

"Yes, yes, yes. Very well, Gar-feen, when are you coming to supper again? My wife says you speak better French than anyone else she knows."

"That's because she's secretly in love with me. Tell her to be brave and patient. I shall come for her one day when you're on duty and we'll elope together to the Paradise Islands."

The thought of his two-hundred-and-thirty pound wife eloping with anybody was too much for him. I depressed the receiver to cut off the sound of his enormous guffaw and dialled a new number.

"Ullo," I said, in my best pea-soup English. "Ees Meestair Gerald Arstlee at 'ome, please?"

"Non, monsieur," Beaver face said. "And neethar is Meeseez Raimington. Adieu." She hung up. I was beginning to hate her. I hate all middle-aged women who try to be smart cookies.

I opened the desk drawer, took out some paper fasteners and an eraser, then put them away again because the feel of the rubber made me think of my kidneys which immediately began to ache. It was getting dark. I opened the safe to see if there were any forgotten bottles and there weren't, so I sat down and got really sore for the next twenty minutes. When I had worked up a real lather I put on the silly fur coat, locked the office, went down to the street, flagged a cab and told the driver to take me to Mornington Drive. The snow was whipping against the windshield. The cold was so intense that the streetcars slipped down every gradient through lack of traction. On days like this it would be more comfortable, and certainly safer, if the city used teams of huskies and sleds.

Up on the mountain it was colder still. I paid off the cabbie and ran up the drive with the icy air burning my lungs. I let myself into the foyer with a gasp of relief and rang the bell. The beavery maid didn't have time to slam the door in my face. I kept right on going, mushing across the lush carpet and straight through the door I had entered the night before, closing it behind me. She was sitting on the same settee, reading what looked like the same shiny magazine. The only difference was that she looked more beautiful. The almost tragic expression on her face suited her classic features to perfection.

I reached into my pocket and pulled out the piece of pasteboard. I said: "I've brought back Junior's picture. Did you want it?"

She stretched out a hand and took it, not speaking, biting her underlip, avoiding my gaze. She had the face of an actress and she might have been acting. I continued, more sharply.

66

"I had a talk with your husband this morning. Interesting man. Fascinating man! He gave me three hundred bucks to close your account with me. Did you want that, too?"

"Please, Mr. Garfin," she whispered. "Go away and leave me alone."

"If you're sure you want that."

"I do want it." She was wringing her hands again, like the night before. It looked almost too pat to be true. She said: "I lay awake last night, thinking of what I had done. I behaved foolishly when I hired you. I was worried and distraught. I was magnifying things out of all proportion; otherwise I wouldn't have done such a thing. I hadn't considered the harm it might do to my husband's reputation if people discovered I was employing a private detective. People talk, Mr. Garfin. They would say all sorts of things."

"And Gerald?"

"I'm sure things will work out all right. He's a good boy at heart. Being his mother, it's only natural that I exaggerate my worries about him."

"As well as his goodness of heart," I said. "Look, Mrs. Remington, there's nobody knows better than I that reputation is a delicate animal. Also that you high muck-amuck mountain folk are greatly given to gossip. All the same I'd like to go on record as having said that your story strikes me as a load of very refined but nevertheless unmitigated cock and bull. What's the truth?"

She stood up with her face like something in marble. "Thank you, that will be all. Good evening."

"A lousy evening," I corrected her. "Cold as charity. And my kidneys hurt where I was beaten up this afternoon."

She stared at me blankly, not flickering a lash. I tried another gambit. "How is Geraldine today? I hope I didn't disturb her too much. That she got a good night's sleep."

Yes, she knew or guessed what had happened. The contempt whisked over her face and was gone immediately.

But that wasn't why I had got my marching papers. The other expression was remaining—a frozen wariness that looked like fear. She said: "Forgive me if I do not care to discuss my family with you."

I whistled through my teeth. I had become the hired help. "Things have changed since yesterday," I said. "You were paying me then to discuss the family. What's happened in between, Mrs. Remington? I have internal bruises that make me want to find out on my own account."

"Leave me alone," she whispered.

"You have a nice husband," I said. "There's probably not a nicer one in Montreal. It's a pity to abuse that lovely confidence he has in you. What are you deceiving him about?"

"Get out!" she said harshly. "I told him to give you two hundred dollars. I understand he gave you three. Is it more money you want? Is that it? Get out! I don't want to be forced to call the police."

"They'd love it," I told her. "But we must think of our reputations. Have I your patrician permission to speak to son Gerald before I go?"

"No," she cried and it sounded like a moan. She turned her back on me and put a steadying hand on the settee. "He isn't here. Please go now. He isn't here."

The door burst open and the smart bitch of a maid came hurtling across the room looking more like a bulldog than the customary beaver. She had a gong-hammer in her hand and appeared about to use it. She opened her mouth for a rallying call that would have brought everybody running for two blocks. I covered her mouth with my hand.

"Take it easy," I said mildly. "I've just told Mrs. Remington an excruciatingly funny joke."

The maid jerked her head and opened her mouth again for a real yell, and Mrs. Remington faced us, completely in control of herself. "Show the gentleman out, Agnes," she commanded icily. "He was just leaving. He will not be calling again."

"With pleasure, ma'am. He won't get in again."

She repeated the last remark with gusto as she slammed the outer door behind me. She underlined it with an ostentatious rattling of bolts.

I was stamping down the drive in the bitter cold, cursing the fact that I'd dismissed the taxi, when I heard the car start up in the garage. I reached the gates and with a muffled roar it came zooming after me. I leapt for the sidewalk and backed against the wall, reaching for the gun that wasn't there, and a glossy Cadillac swerved round the corner and stopped directly opposite me. The inside lights were on and I saw the girl was alone. She opened the door and called my name in a musical voice. I went over and slid in beside her. I had first thought it was Geraldine but I was wrong. It was Marian Remington and she was looking considerably less haughty than she had on the previous night.

"Hello," she said lightly. "If my father had been there he would have asked you to stay to dinner again. Unfortunately he flew to New York this afternoon."

"I'm glad he finally made it," I said.

She had let in the clutch, smoothly for a woman, and we were gliding down the hill. She wasn't looking at me, but her face was smiling. She had a pretty profile.

"Will you," she enquired, "retain a good opinion of the Remington hospitality if I invite you to go with me now to dine at Drury's?"

I thought it over. "I guess I might."

"Then I retain my good opinion of you."

"Why, that's just grand," I said. "But you didn't have to worry. I think you're a wonderful family anyway. My one desire is to get to know all of you a great deal better."

The smile disappeared from her face and I felt her go taut. She pressed the accelerator and the car leapt forward. "No," she said. "No, we're not. About being a wonderful family, I mean. We're not. That's really why I'm inviting you to dinner.

I hope you don't mind. I want to tell you about it."

I looked at her closely. I hadn't realised before how very young she was.

# 8

It was pleasant. We sat in a corner with the waiters pussy-footing over to us and the soft music piping gently through. She insisted upon everything: the martinis, the Bordeaux and the brandy: the hors d'oeuvres, the escargots, the beef and the crêpe suzettes. The works. And meantime she occasionally brushed me under the table with her knee, lightly and accidentally, encouraging me to think that later I could repay the compliment. She wasn't at all the same girl tonight. She looked less like her father. Her dark hair, brushed until it gleamed like silk, was pushed back over small pink ears, each wearing a diamond stud-button that would have kept me in comfort for six months. Her eyes were softer, a darker grey, and she was practicing an eyelid fluttering trick that made the long lashes sweep down over her cheek. She wasn't exactly warm because the family chastity remained in her face, cool now rather than cold. But what the hell, I thought. There comes a time in every man's life when a little purity makes a refreshing change.

And she seemed willing. She was vamping me and doing it well, and I liked it. I also wondered what we were leading up to. I sat munching my dessert and trying to scheme up a foolproof theme.

She said prettily: "That's a lovely coat you're wearing tonight."

"Don't be witty. I'm changing back to last night's tweed just as soon as I get home."

"But I knew you weren't a decorator. You're not a bit like one."

"What does everyone have against decorators?"

She smiled. Her teeth were beautiful. "For that matter," she mused on, "you're not a bit like a detective, either, not the ones I've read about. I expected you to call me 'baby' and say that I was a 'Ritzy dame.' It's exactly what I am, you know. Exactly. A Ritzy dame. But you're positively respectful to women."

"It's always been my main failing."

"It makes me regret how rude I was to you last night."

"Only a little," I said. "But last night you didn't want anything from me. Tonight you do. What is it?"

"Now who's being rude?" She did the trick with her eyelids again and her nice teeth chewed gently on her lower lip. "Be patient with me," she said. "I'm sitting here trying to work up the courage to say what I have to say. Can we talk about something else for a while? Art or music or something?"

"Okay. Who was Garcia Lorca?"

"A rather wonderful poet who was executed by Franco's men during the Spanish civil war. Why, have you read him?"

"I believe he was recently quoted to me," I said. "Some very fetching stuff. Quite descriptive."

"Oh, I see," she said drily. "You've met my stepsister. His work contains one of her favourite passages. Geraldine has a positive genius for skimming through the classics and extracting anything that might be construed as pornographic. Did she read you any of the Shakespeare sonnets? She has an interpretation of some of them that would curl Shakespeare's celestial hair. Her notion of the ideal Christmas present is the complete and unexpurgated works of Henry Miller."

I made a mental note of Henry Miller. "I like Geraldine," I said. "She seems to have a very warm nature."

"Most men think so. I loathe her. She's a dirty nasty little bitch of a nymphomaniac, and she makes me sick."

"Whew!" I went tch tch. "But now you'll find it easier to tell me what you want, won't you?"

She looked at me with narrow eyes. "You know, you're clever," she said. "Cleverer than I thought. Yes, I'll tell you. I want you to protect my father's name from anything the Astleys may do. Especially my stepmother."

"She's not an Astley, dear, she's a Remington," I said. "Don't let jealousy run away with you. I noticed it last night at the dinner table."

Instantly she sobered, looked serious. "Is it so obvious? I suppose it is. I try not to be, I try to like her, but she's made it impossible—she and those ghastly children of hers." She brushed a hand against her forehead and made a rueful mouth. "Poor Daddy, it's useless for me to tell him. He won't hear a word against her. That's why I've come to you. I want you to get proof."

"Of what?"

"I believe my stepmother has a lover."

"A lot of married women have," I said. "So what, so long as your father is happy?"

She contemplated me with the old contempt she had used on her stepbrother. "Alley-cat morality," she said.

"Mink," I corrected. "Minky Mike Garfin they call me."

"That's not amusing."

"It wasn't meant to be. I'm sorry, I don't take the sort of job you're offering."

"Not for good money?"

"No."

"Not for forty dollars a day?"

"You're vicious as well as jealous," I said. "Okay, for forty a day I'll take it."

"You're mercenary as well as pseudo-noble," she rejoined.

"My prices may go up in a couple of days."

"I think I'm expecting it." She studied the fingernails of her right hand, then looked up smiling. "And now we've got the insults out of our systems can we go back to being pleasant again?"

"Your wish is my command, boss," I said. I lit a cigarette, offering her one which she refused. "Tell me, how do you get on with stepbrother Gerald?"

She thought deeply, puckered her cute forehead. "I suppose he's all right, basically. Anyway, he's the least harmful of the three. Now and then he gets drunk and a bartender phones and advises me to pick him up, but he's always fairly discreet about it. I think Daddy might make a man of Gerald if his mother didn't dote on him and try to cover up everything he does. If she were more open we could at least persuade him to do his drinking at hime and stop disappearing on those week-long bats of his."

"You puritans," I said, "don't understand about drinking. Does he disappear often?"

"Every six weeks or so. He's on one now, I think. He didn't come home last night."

And then it was that the brandy turned acid in my mouth and started frying my tongue. The thought of Death came and stood at my back—Death as the individual, the tangible person who had once followed me through the undergrowth of the upper Quebec forest, never more than six feet away, for the three whole days that I was lost in the green wilderness.

It was ridiculous. It was stupid bog-Irish superstition. I looked around the restaurant—the carpet, the discreet diners, the dark wood of the bar, the glinting cocktail shaker thrashing the air. It was no use. The thing was over my shoulder and I was icy cold. And suddenly I felt the need for someone—someone warm whose presence would prove that I was alive; not this cool, antiseptic virgin sitting opposite me, chaste and chill as the wind that whirled the snow along the streets outside. I needed a moistness, a heat, something that would throw off this dry cold hand that was laid on my shoulder. I needed Tessie.

"Let's go," I said and got to my feet. She came with me, looking perplexed, forgetting to nod to the bowing waiters as she had done when we entered. Outside in the vestibule, as we put on our coats, she asked where we were going.

"I," I said, "not you. I have an appointment." But I was feeling better already.

"I'll drop you," she said.

"No thanks. Matter of fact, my car's parked just down the road."

"Oh." She shifted from one foot to the other, seemingly disappointed, as if she had expected to make a night of it. "I'll call at your office tomorrow and pay you a retainer," she said. "You have agreed to take the job, haven't you?"

"Yes," I answered, and took her out and put her in the car, not talking.

She smiled up at me from behind the wheel. "You know you're just a little bit strange."

"I know." I slammed the door and waved and watched her drive away into the white and swirling night. Then I went over to the cab stand and got in the front one and told the driver to take me to Tessie's.

It was the dark and luscious Marguerite who answered the door, wearing a soft, sated invisible bloom like wild plum at night. "Where is Tom?" she sighed softly to me. "Where is that great hairy animal?"

"I thought he was here."

"He came," she said. "He went." She gave a languid wave of the hand.

"Tell me."

"And they call him Littlejohn. Was there ever a man had such a wrong name?" She held her hands in front of her and went down the passage to the sitting-room in a burlesque sleepwalking pose. "It will never be the same again," she said. "Nothing will. Will it, honey?"

Tessie looked up from her needlework. She has a passion, among other things, for making pictures in silk which afterwards she frames. The apartment walls are full of them—the Santa Maria, the Cows at Dee, all bright and gay and arty-tarty. "I can only go by hearsay," she said. "He was certainly cute. But this one's my one."

She took a look at me and saw how things were and got rid of her needle. "Sorry you have to go out, Marguerite. Goodbye, dear." She waved a gently dismissing hand.

"The trouble with you two," Marguerite said, "is that you lack refinement. A gentle little hint would have been more proper." She giggled a bit, pulling on her ermiline coat and ramming a piece of fur on her head. "I shall be at Madame Forgue's. Call me the instant that thing comes back. We'll make a foursome."

"Don't catch cold, Maggie," I called as she went out.

Tessie went over to the liquor cabinet and poured us both a drink. I took off my coat and jacket and dropped them on the floor. It seemed a good idea so I dropped myself on the floor. The carpet wasn't as thick as the Remingtons', but I liked it better. Tessie came and sat beside me and we drank our drinks and I laid my head on her lap. She began stroking my hair. I guess I'll never get a secretary. It takes a long time for a woman to learn exactly the right way a man likes his head stroked. Then, too, a secretary might not have her own apartment. Then, too, she certainly wouldn't have Tessie's taste in liquor.

"You're a nice girl, Tess," I said.

She bent over and kissed me, not answering, keeping herself close and studying my face. "You in trouble?"

"I don't know."

"Tell me about it."

"Wait till Tom gets here."

She said: "Is it something to do with that kid who should have come here last night?"

"Maybe. I think so."

"If I can be of any help." She kissed me again. I went from a warm seventh heaven up to the sixty-ninth. Twenty minutes later, pondering our second drink, she said, "You really are a satisfactory type."

"So I've been told."

She pushed back her yellow mane and looked at me with narrow eyes. "Who've you been mixing with lately?"

"Jealous?"

"Yes."

I put my arms around her.

And after a while—"Marguerite is developing one of those things for your pal Tom. I hope he gets back soon."

"Me too," I said. "He has my car. I'll not wait past midnight. I need sleep. Badly. And I wouldn't get any with you."

"Whose fault?" she asked. We both thought that was funny.

So I waited until midnight and he didn't show. At one o'clock Marguerite came in, disappointed we hadn't called her, more disappointed that he wasn't with us. I stayed until two, and then half-past. Still he hadn't shown. Finally I called a cab and went out into the freezing night.

The driver said it was twenty-eight below zero, and I believed him. The snow had ceased and the air was brittle as mica. For the first time I was glad the Youth's Companion had given me the fur coat. I wondered how Tom was faring in the tweed, and hoped he'd have sense enough to put the car somewhere under cover for the night.

Then as I pulled out my key it occurred to me that he might have been in bed since ten o'clock, sleeping off last night's liquor and the afternoon's bout. I opened the front door, kicked over the milk bottles, set them up and went into my sitting room, standing a while to let the warmth restore me to normal. The Lindsay had made up a bed on the settee obviously for me. I crossed the passage to the bedroom and saw she had made up my bed just as obviously for Tom. She was using her highly prized and rarely used padded quilt and there was a bottle of Scotch and a siphon on the bedside table. The boy was a smash hit.

But he wasn't there. I cracked the Scotch, not using the siphon, and sat around trying to figure the switch in my new job. The Remington girl was pretty. Her step-mother was handsome. They were in fact a good-looking family and, apart from sexual aberrations, probably nice people if only they could get rid of the little jealousies and mild fears they had for each other. Or, for that matter, of the idolising love some of them bore for the others. I had another drink and decided it was a perfectly straight-forward job. Except for the little matter of being beaten up this afternoon. Almost killed.

Well, to hell with Tom. If he was going to be late he could have the settee. I undressed slowly, took a last drink and got into bed. I lay awake a while, reflecting how simple life would be if only people would refrain from jealousies. I am half Irish, so this type of thought comes to me whether I like it or not.

I closed my eyes then and went to sleep immediately and was catapulted into a series of pretty horrible dreams. I awoke several times, sweating. Once I called out.

# 9

The thickly frosted windows couldn't keep out the brilliant sunlight that filled the morning. I awoke with it in my eyes.

There was a gentle tap on my bedroom door and the Lindsay's voice said liltingly: "Half-past eight, laddie. A nice hot plate of porridge waiting for you. Hurry now."

"No," I snarled. "I loathe and despise porridge. And this is me. Your laddie had to sleep on the settee."

She pushed the door open and marched in. "Don't let

77

envy get the upper hand," she said briskly. "And he's not on the settee. I was in there first."

"Then he spent the night with some broad."

Miss Lindsay looked interested. "A broad? Is that comfortable?"

"Very. Now get out. I want to dress."

"Don't fuss. The porridge will be cold. Put on a dressing gown. And hurry. Sir Walter Scott is acting mist peculiar this morning. I want you to have a look at him."

I got out of bed, remembering my back as suddenly it rubbed the rime from the inside of the outer ones and peered through to take in the day. The reflection of sun on snow was almost blinding. My car was standing directly in front, with that peculiar frozen stiff look that cars get after a cold night. I hoped it wouldn't be a garage job.

I crossed to the sitting room. There was no place Tom could have fallen, and no hiding place except behind the settee. He wasn't there. I returned to the bedroom and looked through the window again. He wasn't in the car, either, unless he were slumped down. And, no, he was too large. The car wasn't big enough. I washed my hands and went down to the kitchen, thinking it all a poor joke. The table was set with a steaming plate of oats, which I didn't want. I ate them because it pleased the Lindsay, and asked for some ham and eggs.

"Have you noticed Sir Walter?" she asked.

The cat was standing in a corner, an awkward pose, its back slightly arched and the impression that it was about to stand on tip-toe. It was staring at the back door.

"Here, you," I said. He didn't move. "Here, Sir Walter Scott," I said, and put a piece of hot buttered toast on the floor, a delicacy the Lindsay has taught him to appreciate. He remained rigid, not deviating the line of his gaze by a hairbreadth. "Anyone outside?" I asked.

She shook her head. "I peeped out. The silly thing is having a daft half-hour."

"Unrealisable lust," I told her. "You should never have had done to him what you did."

She put the ham and eggs in front of me, making scanalised noises, and I started eating. And it was then the cat began softly to yowl, opening its red mouth, not moving its body, pouring forth a continuous tiny ululation that made the downy hairs on my spine rise up like spikes. I didn't like it. I got up and rattled the handle of the inner door. "Come on, Scott," I said. "Go for a prowl."

He should have come scampering. He didn't. He remained immobile. Yowling.

I opened the inner door and rattled the outer, knowing already that he wasn't going to move. Then I opened the outer door and the freezing air filled the kitchen and wrapped around me, and because I could no longer help it I stepped outside onto the back porch and looked down the garden.

Tom was sitting down at the end, with his back to the fence. He wasn't moving. I saw he would not be moving again, not ever. He looked so bitterly, bitterly cold.

The tweed coat was hung negligently like a cloak over his shoulders. One skirt had frozen to the fence. His eyes were tight shut and his mouth was slightly open and his head was tilted back so that it rested against a post. His necktie was loosened and his coat and shirt were unbuttoned so that his chest was showing.

I walked towards him. I didn't touch him. I stood and stared. There wasn't a trace of color in all his flesh. His ears were stark white and brittle, as if they would disintegrate at the touch of a finger. His arms were flung open helplessly, hopelessly, with the great hands dead on the frozen earth. His shut eyes were fringed with frost. His hair was a whitened mat. I stared at him and shivered in the cold and wept in grief and fury with tears that froze on my face as they fell. I guess I might have stayed there all day if Miss Lindsay hadn't led me back to the house, murmuring how I'd catch my death of cold and pinching fiercely the back of my hand to shock some sense into me. In the kitchen the cat still moaned its weird noises. She picked it up and began petting it to quietness.

She said to me: "Are you all right? I don't want you to be. If I don't have you to fuss over I don't know what I shall do. He was such a braw laddie, yon one. Such a bonnie thing."

I went back down to the garden and removed all the papers from Tom's pockets. Then I came back and called Captain Masson. I said: "Which medic is on duty this morning?"

"Dr. Armand. He won't cure your belly-ache. He doesn't like you well enough."

"Can you get Bertrand?"

"No."

"Listen," I said. "There's a guy sitting in my garden with not a mark on him. He's been murdered. I want to know how and I want to know quick. Send the boys to collect him and use every ounce of pressure to make Armand carry out an immediate autopsy."

"I don't have any pressure."

"For God's sake work some up."

"Okay, Michel," he said quietly. "If it's like that. Rely on me, Michel. I'll do it."

I hung up and went straightaway and took a hot bath. I wanted to avoid the questions, the photographers, the experts, the whole bloody bunch of vultures that goes with these jobs. It was impossible of course. I couldn't leave Lindsay to their tender mercies. So I went out eventually and took another look at him. I watched them snip away his frozen hair from the post. I listened while they complained of the difficulty they had getting him into the wagon because of the position into which he'd been frozen.

A small crowd of vampires had materialised from no-where on the back street and were sucking up the spectacle with hungry eyes. I kept my hands in my pockets and prayed childishly that they would die of slow and filthy diseases. He had been drunk, they said. Dead drunk he must have been. The woman over there with the pinched nose and rimless spectacles would probably tell all about it at her next meeting of the WCTU. I kept my mouth shut, not answering any questions. I climbed into the back of the wagon when they were ready to go and sat near the bunched up thing that had been Tom. Grown men, they say, don't have such emotions. Grown men do. I sat with the tips of my fingers touching his frozen head and vowed to do slow murder to avenge this one. My hatred was an agony that consumed my insides. My horror and shame were like a hot iron across my brain. I had done this first to Danny Menzies. And now to Tom. The Three Musketeers!

"Someone you know?" the attendant asked, grinning. "You ought to warn your pals not to drink on cold nights."

I spat in his face.

## 10

Someone told Dr. Armand that I was concerned in it. He came sliding into Masson's office about five minutes after my arrival and started protesting in his yapping little voice. This, he yelped, was not the proper routine. He was busy, he had other work to do. Where was Frankisson? He wanted to make a complaint. And who—with a hostile sidelong look at me—was running this department, anyway?

"Still whining?" I said.

"Shut your damn mouth, you." He blazed into anger and beat his fist on Masson's desk. "I want to see Frankisson."

Masson remained stolid. "Impossible. Frankisson has gone to St. Agathe for the day. We can't get in touch with him."

"While the cat's away the mice behave like rats," Armand sneered.

"Witty," I said. I'd have put him out of commission if he hadn't been needed.

"That'll be all, Doctor," Masson said. "The autopsy is an emergency. Do as you have been requested."

Armand was white with temper. "If I had to do this for every drunken bastard who fell down in the streets—"

I got to my feet. "Push!" I said. He took a look at me and pushed, slamming the door furiously behind him.

Masson shook his head. "There are times, Michel, when you are more Irish than French," he said. "All the same, it is lucky that Frankisson chose today to go out of town. He would have liked seeing you here."

"The police department is stacked with friends of mine," I said sarcastically.

Masson grinned ruefully. He was nervous himself at having taken on so much authority. "And was the man drunk?"

"No."

"Who was he?"

"I'd like to leave it until I hear what Armand says."

Masson shrugged.

His office had a mixed odor of chalk and ink. When Armand returned—after nearly three hours of taking his sweet and vindictive time—the smell had reduced me to the frustrated mental state of a schoolboy being kept in after hours. The doctor came round the door with a couple of papers in his hand and a satisfied smirk playing around the gashy little purse of his mouth. He leaned against the desk, blinking at me slowly, like a crocodile. Something was causing him to enjoy himself, right to the full of his miserable little soul. He really did hate my guts. He said:

"A remarkable resemblance. For a few blissful moments in there I imagined it was you. Promise you'll show me some time how it's done."

"Finish that," Masson growled. "Fight it out somewhere else. What did you find?"

Armand was still grinning, eyebrows up. "A relation of yours, then? Let me offer my deepest condolences. These family bereavements—"

I took his lapel between thumb and forefinger. "You're a very funny man for an abortionist," I said gently. "I'm fighting the temptation to kick your backbone up through your scalp."

"Sit down, Garfin," Masson snapped.

Armand rustled his papers triumphantly. "He's tough," he said. "Exceedingly tough. But one shot and they're all tough, aren't they? Only your chum took one too many. I find that extremely droll. His sleigh ride was so smooth that he thought he was in bed. So he undressed himself. At thirty below. Oh yes, extremely droll. Ha ha!"

"Sleigh ride?" Masson asked. "That true?"

"Sure it is," Armand sneered. "And so's this bastard. Look at his eyes. Crazy. Hopped to the gills. There's a law against it in this province. Put him under arrest and I'll be only too happy conduct the examination."

"I bet you would." I took his arm and closed my hand. I was shaking. I said: "Cut the humor and tell me what I want to know."

"See that? You see?" The little rat's voice went way up. He was getting frightened. Maybe I looked bad. "The two of them were on a hopfest last night. I'll stake my reputation on it."

"For God's sake, cut it out!" Masson snapped. "Sit down, Michel. Give me the official report, you."

Armand threw the papers and they drifted down onto the desk. The sneer was back on his face. "It's all there," he said. "A main-liner who couldn't quite make it home. There was enough heroin in him to supply a normal dopester for a week—if there are any normal dopesters. The world's better without him. The world would be better without all of them."

"Wouldn't that leave you a little short of cash, Doctor?" Masson asked drily. Armand shut up with a snap like a goosed oyster. The captain picked up the papers

"Contusion on the back of the head," he read, "probably caused by violent contact with the fencepost."

"With a blackjack," I said. "Before the dope was administered."

"Administered!" Armand tittered with derision. "That's very good. Ha, ha!"

I was having trouble keeping my hands off him. I picked up the phone from the desk. "All right?" I asked.

"Go ahead."

I dialled the number, keeping my eyes on Armand. The little swine made me sick and even at a time like this I couldn't resist the getting at him. When someone answered at the other end, I asked for Collis and was put through. He came on sounding smooth and urbane; then he realised who I was and the pig-iron came into his voice. He wasn't going to like me any better when I'd finished my piece.

"They have one of your boys stretched out on a slab down at the morgue," I said. "RCMP Sergeant Tom Little-John from Alberta. He's been murdered. I hope I can convince you of that. There's a certain Dr. Armand here who claims it was death by misadventure. He tells me some of the Mounted Police are habitual drug addicts. You'll find it in his official report."

Armand made a snatch at the phone and I knocked him to the other end of the room. He looked fit-frightened and he had cause to be. If I knew the Mounties, that official report was going to haunt him for the rest of his short career. I noticed that Masson was sliding the papers into his desk. I liked that.

From the other end of the phone came a long silence, then, "Are you mixed up in this, Garfin?" The words fell like broken beer bottles.

"In a way," I answered. "I'm holding his papers. Should I give them to the City Police?"

"And then come over. I want to see you."

Old habit is hard to break. I said, "Yes, sir," and hung up. I turned to Armand. "Right, my friend. It was that Collis. He's going to remember you after your report has gone through. Every Mountie in the country will remember you. And you may have heard—they always get their man."

"You scummy bastard," he snarled, and he was trembling. "You son of a bitch's son." I didn't hit him. It would have spoiled the enjoyment. I merely imitated his original smirk and gave it back.

Masson got to his feet. He didn't look pleased himself, maybe even a little bit scared. "What's the idea?" he demanded quietly. "You can think of more ways of making yourself unpopular."

"Sorry," I said, and I meant it. It was a lousy trick to have played on him. But had I got in touch with the Mounties right away, it would have been the end so far as I was concerned. They would have shut the door in my face. I could no more have squeezed information out of them than marrow out of a bone. And this was a personal matter.

As it was, I had a clue. A skimpy one, but a clue. Narcotics.

I handed over the papers I had taken from Tom's jacket and left the station. The sun was brilliant, the snow glittering. I tried to brighten, but was unsuccessful. I was thinking of the coming interview with Collis, which wasn't going to be pleasant. I was thinking too that it was I who had put the finger on Tom and signed his death warrant. I had killed him to save myself. The least I could do now was to—

# 11

Collis had a rectangular military face with a clipped moustache, salt and pepper hair and a faint smell of leather about him. He spoke to me as if he were turning something over with the toe of his shiny shoe. I had told him all I knew, including why I had blatted Tom's name, and now as he put down the phone I was thinking that he hadn't believed a word I said. I didn't blame him. There was no reason why he should.

He said: "I needn't keep you any longer. My men have checked all you told me. The Romilly Club was open until eight o'clock this morning, and the City Police are going to prosecute for infringement of the liquor laws. The main point, however, is that Jean Genet, the proprietor, was present at all times, as was an entertainer named William Cardy, a dwarf who does tumbling tricks. In the upstairs apartment a poker game was in progress, lasting until almost noon today. Among those in unbroken attendance were two brothers named Starkie and a large man who gives his name as Waterford. There are impartial witnesses, willing to testify under oath."

"They'd have their alibis fixed anyway," I said. "Although I'm fairly convinced they had nothing to do with it, except for spreading the word of Tom's identity."

Collis smiled bleakly. "They all deny having heard of him. Or you."

"They would."

He leaned forward, bending his ramrod back. "Garfin, who killed Littlejohn?"

"Your guess is better than mine," I said. "They used heroin. Doesn't that indicate it was done by the boys he was tracking down?"

"Boys? Tracking down?"

"Come off," I said. "He was on a narcotics case."

The back straightened with a jerk. He assumed the deadpan No-Information expression that a Mountie gets issued with his first uniform. "Indeed?"

"Yes, indeed. Who was he trailing? I have a hankering to continue to search myself."

He pressed his finger tips hard on the desk. His jaw went like rock. "That will be the job of this Force, Garfin," he said. "I believe you once had the opportunity to be one of us. Your assistance is no longer needed. You may go now."

It was a dirty crack and I was surprised it could still hurt. I got up and went to the door, not saying anything. He spoke again. "I'm afraid you'll be unable to use your car for another week. It had been towed to headquarters for checking."

I knew a week was unnecessary. They would do it in a matter of hours. But Collis enjoyed taking that last jab, and somehow it made me feel better. He seemed more human. I flipped my hat, went down the corridor, continued along the avenue of flatly hostile eyes that lined the main room, and got out into the street. I looked at my watch and was surprised to find the interview had lasted less than two hours. To me it had been ten years. I glanced over my shoulder at headquarters and wished for one disemboweling moment that I was back among the guys inside, working with the solid weight of authority behind me. But the perplexity behind Collis's rigid face indicated that for the time being he knew as little as I did, and not all the authority in the world would give him a lead toward solving the case. Leads are got by one method only—legwork. I turned east along St. Catherine and started walking. I walked ten blocks, dodged three more, backed on my tracks, and finally got rid of the guy who was tailing me. He was young and amateurish. I guess he was a rookie. I wish I could have let him stay longer, to give him heart, but this was a personal matter. I walked on alone.

I worked it systematically. I started on Dorchester Street with some one-night rooming houses that I knew from past experience. I didn't have much hope, and I was right. All they offered me was a bed. I carried on south and through to the waterfront area, combing flop-houses and drifting in and out of taverns. I saw just one addict, out stone cold on a twenty-five cent bed. I couldn't wake him and I doubt he could have told me anything even if he'd been in full possession of his senses. The area was dead, the harbor frozen over. There were no ships coming in, and even the crummiest member of the narcotics traffic had moved uptown for bigger profits.

I beat my way back to Chinatown, getting fed up but sticking to the system. Johnny Ching was in back of his plush restaurant, playing fantan with a bunch of the boys. Johnny and I are friends of long standing. Time was, years ago, when he ran an opium parlor, but stricter laws, cumbersome equipment, and the fact that you can smell the greasy stink of opium for about six blocks, have long since made past history of the profession. No, Johnny couldn't tell me a thing. He no longer even knew anyone in narcotics. He was now, he told me, a respectable 'restauranteur,' and I could see he got a kick out of saying the word. He also wanted to get back to his game of fantan, because he was winning. We shook hands and said goodbye.

Out in the street the darkness was falling. I looked at my watch and walked faster. It was time now to hit St. Lawrence Main, after dark.

The evening had begun to crawl. The night birds were emerging form their little nests. The movie-cum-striptease joints had their lights on, and the barkers were out front hollering that we were all just in time to see this week's extrah-speshul show. In the doorways, and peering from the pinball saloons, the earliest birds gathered: the straight drunks; the alcoholics trying to bum the price of one; the fags hoping for something quick with the guys coming home from work; the superannuated whores hoping for something at any speed with anyone who had fifty cents; the pencil-moustached pimps in fedoras, casing the crowd for guys who looked like they had five dollars, because flashy headgear costs money and a feller never knows when he might need another hat.

They were standing. They were moving slowly around. Singly. In pairs. In gaggles. All giving out with their brand of come-hither and hoping it would work. All looking as if they might freeze to death in this bitter weather if they stayed too long. All looking warmer than Tom.

I moved on. Slowly. A pusher I knew slipped into a door. I followed him down to an empty basement where four teen-age kids were waiting with their tongues hanging out and dollar bills clutched tightly in their hot little hands. Marijuana. Any petty punk can peddle marijuana. It's grown in the city. Consequently—no lead.

I climbed back onto the street and went on to a place I knew that had been in operation a few months before. It still was. The funny thing about habituals is that no matter what brand they use or dangers they run, they all like to cling together, to have parties, to stick to their old haunts. This place was going full swing. But there was nobody I knew well enough to pump for information, and a question out of place in a joint like that finds you ending up in a cement mixer. I mushed on.

It was cold. It was after six o'clock and I hadn't eaten since breakfast so I decided to kill two birds with one stone. There are several large restaurants in Montreal East where cokies and pushers meet for trade. I headed for the nearest— two acres in size and greasy as a cold pork chop. I ordered coffee and six sinkers and sat down to watch. Someone should have wiped the rim of my cup. I had to do it myself.

I first saw the kid without really noticing him. He was

maybe twenty years old, with mousy hair and a pinched, twitching nose, a real dug-out, scraping the bottom. If he'd ever had any decent clothes he'd long since sold them for a sniff at the cokie. He was in need of another right now, and badly. I didn't dwell on him. What's the use?

On my fourth sinker my eyes skidded to him again. I recognised him behind what had happened since. Purely for interest, I went over and sat beside him. He didn't blink.

I said: "How's Gerald Astley? I haven't seen him in a long time."

His eyes remained glassy. He was staring past my shoulder at nothing. He opened his mouth and his teeth were shot to hell. His voice rustled like dry leaves.

"I don't know you. Buck off!"

"But I know you," I said, friendly. "I saw you play football once and I remember you ran a good game. It was the afternoon you and Gerald had your picture taken together."

"That fruit," he said tonelessly.

"I thought you were pals."

He came vaguely to life. He looked as if he might cry. "I thought so too until the last time I saw him. He wouldn't give me a nickel. Pushed me into the gutter. Pansy!"

"When was that?"

He came too much to life. He went suddenly crafty. "What's that to you?"

I shrugged. I said: "You still at McGill?"

"Like this? That's a laugh."

"What happened? Exams?"

"I didn't know it would turn out this way," he said. "I took just a little pinch to help get through the Maths paper." The irony of it must have struck him. He laughed almost sanely. "Imagine anyone wanting to get through a Maths paper."

I said: "Want some coffee?"

He looked at me hungrily, starting to shimmer. "You know what I want. I want it bad."

I took out a two-dollar bill and put it on the table with my hand over it. "How long since you told the truth?"

He licked his dry lips. "Ask me anything."

"Was Gerald Astley a cokie?"

"No."

"Did he supply your coke?"

He shook his head. "No."

I took out another two dollars. "You get this as well if you can truthfully say that he did."

The head nodded violently. "That's right, I remember he did. He used to bring it on the campus and—"

He was lying through his teeth. I withdrew the money and he reached out and clutched my wrist. "Okay." he said. "You know goddam well he didn't so what are we playing at?"

I pushed over the money. "Did he suggest the first sniff?"

"No."

The cokie had the money in his pocket and he turned into a big man. Crafty. Tough. An equal. He said: "You're interested in Gerald Astley, and it so happens that I know all about him. Some very interesting things. Some very interesting answers to questions you haven't even asked me. Give me five hundred and I'll tell."

"Beat it," I said. "I'm busy." I meant it. Gerald Astley didn't figure in Tom's murder. He would have to wait until this other matter was cleared up, and maybe not even then. His mother was no longer hiring me. She was the watched one now, not the client. I thought of Marian Remington and wondered if she'd waited long at the office today to pay me that retainer. Maybe she was mad. Maybe I'd kissed the forty a day goodbye.

So I had. So what?

So having spent four useful bucks and ten useless minutes

on the cokie I got up and walked out. He was still muttering his snifty dream about selling me this information. I took no notice. The day had vanished fast, and apart from a couple of unpleasant sights I was right where I had been in the cold morning. I threaded through the shivering, slip-slithering crowds on the sidewalk, trying to figure where I'd go next.

Then I saw Snowy Etheridge. He was way ahead of me and I could only see his straight back, his high-held head, but I knew who it was by the way people were turning to give him that second admiring look. Snowy is, as they say, a right handsome guy. He's thirty but you'd think he was twenty. He has that wry, slightly bashful outdoor look that women adore and men admire—tall, crisp-looking, bright blue eyes and chestnut hair. He has big shoulders and a virile way of walking. He is probably the most unprincipled, unmoral rat in the entire city.

Snowy isn't plain rotten; he transcends anything so ordinary. All you have to do when dealing with him is to stretch your imagination to the fabulous worst and then expect it of him, and more. He'll come through. And don't ever say, do, or even think anything on which he can make money, because Snowy would drown his mother in her own milk for a nickel. The only faint chink in his armor is that he's superstitious. Black cars, ladders and Friday the thirteenth he doesn't like because no one has paid him to. He goes in for having his fortune told, weekly, and I've heard say he's afraid of a dark room. He'd been useful to me and he's cost me plenty. His fees come high when he has what you want. On purely moral grounds, and for the good of the community, Snowy should be exterminated.

There's a story about him to the effect that when he was eighteen he started pushing, rolled his own pellets, and forgot to plug his nostril with cotton wool. That, they say, is how Snowy got the habit. You'd never know it to look at him. Not a twitch.

He turned into a small, respectable cafe, followed by the gazes of six women and one fat man—who was probably fooling himself that once he used to look like that. I got alongside and looked through the window. A waitress was already putting in front of him a cup of coffee and a plate of something.

I reached for the door and a hand grabbed my arm and pulled me back. The cokie had followed me from the other dump. He must have moved fast. The passers-by were looking at him with disdain and at me with sympathy. He looked a bum all right. He said:

"I'll tell you for three hundred."

"Beat it," I said.

"Two hundred."

He was prepared to stick with me all night. I reached into a pocket and gave him one of my cards. "Call me later," I said. "I'm busy." I didn't wait to see him go. I pushed open the door and walked in.

Snowy had the cup to his mouth. I walked up behind him and touched him lightly on the shoulder and said quietly, "Hello, Snowy."

He turned around casually, and then he jerked like a pulled puppet and the coffee went all over his lap. He was bug-ging at me. He was dead white. He was paralysed with fright.

And then it dawned on my dumb brain and I ran across the cafe and out of the door, crashing through the passers-by to get to the middle of the street and a better view of both sides, both ways. I stood poised on my toes, ready, until the streetcars got tired of banging their bells and threatened to run me down. It was no use. The cokie had disappeared. There were four dollars in his jeans and a dozen side-streets and two dozen houses into which he might have gone. He was probably already snuggled down.

I returned to the café. The waitress had finished mop-ing Snowy's lap. She gave me a dirty look for daring to soil such a nice young man, and retreated to her counter. I sat down. He was completely recovered.

I said: "What made you think I was dead?"

He grinned. "For how much?"

"Okay," I said. "I'll be finding out anyway."

"A sensible attitude. Now go away. I'm expecting a friend for a private conversation."

I tried to look uninterested. "It won't be worth it," I said, "but how much do you say?"

I was fooling no one. The grin widened. "Two hundred."

"Forty."

"We're agreed on a hundred and twenty."

"Okay," I said.

"A party last night. There was a joke being told that someone had filled you up and left you out in the damp night air without your knickers. Hellishly funny. Even the people who didn't know you were laughing. Somebody brought the story from another party and I don't know who it was. I don't know where the other party was, either. Raise the ante to five hundred and I'll find out. Otherwise, one hundred and twenty. Now."

"For that?"

"You made the deal."

I took out my wallet and paid him. A fat-faced man who was standing by the counter grinned, came over and sat down. "Hi, Snowy," he said. "Glad ta see youse is pals. This geezer was follering yer. It was funny. Some little gapper was follering him. They had a chat."

"Where'd he go?" I said. Too quickly. Snowy's eyes gleamed and the other guy's fat face shut up like a bank safe. "That's fine," I said. "It's not important. So long, Snowy. See you again when I feel philanthropic."

"Do that." Snowy pocketed the money and turned away, no longer interested. Or seeming not to be. I was willing to bet a pound of nuts that he was fascinated. I wondered in how many seconds after I left the place he would begin to move. He had thought I was dead. That meant other people thought I was dead and somebody had made a mistake. Snowy would be seeing if there were dividends in rectifying the error.

## 12

Me! They had meant to kill me. And this brought Gerald Astley right back into the picture. Tom's size, his coloring, his resemblance to me—the tweed coat, the maroon coupé with the doorkeeper bending over it. Maybe he was slugged in the dark. But the killer needed some light to inject the morphine. Which meant he knew me so little that even then he didn't realise his error. Going by a description, perhaps. Or someone who had seen me only once.

Further—Snowy Etheridge had learned of my death at a hop party. The news was brought from another party. Dopesters get an extra kick out of taking the stuff in groups, and when the bang is beginning to bang they can't resist bragging about what they've done. The guy who had killed me wasn't bragging, only a little misguided. But to be in the group, and blowing hard, made him an addict.

So—the little guy at Maisie's place with the knife and the fedora. When he saw me he was twitching off the white mosquitoes, which made him a not very acute observer. Also he had seen me for only a few minutes. He seemed to fit the bill.

But why? Reason one; they'd finally discovered I was no longer a Mountie but a nondescript private eye with nobody backing me. Reason two, and the main reason; Gerald Astley. Somehow. Was he tied up with narcotics or was the method of Tom's murder a coincidental eccentricity of the killer? I didn't know. Or care. For the moment I wanted only to get my hands on the guy who'd done the job. Other issues were secondary.

If Gerald Astley's cokie pal had come back at that moment I'd have given him ten thousand dollars and my right arm for his information. I looked along a few streets in the offchance that he was returning to put the bite on me again. He wasn't. With the four bucks already out of his jeans he would be stretched somewhere dreaming his sad dream of temporary power. I flagged a passing cab and climbed in beside the driver.

"Out west and onto Decarie Boulevard."

"Yes, sir."

I knew if I didn't call the police I was headed for further trouble. To hell with them. After this morning they would ask more questions than usual. And doubt more answers. And my friend Frankisson might be back from St. Agathe by now. and most important, if there was a leak at headquarters the little twitcher and his knife would be over the hills two minutes after the warrant was issued.

"Where to exactly, sir?"

The cabbie was calling me 'monsieur' which translates as 'sir' but doesn't mean precisely the same, is less formal. He was young and French-Canadian and had a three-day growth on his cheerful face. He wasn't wearing the weary look that an all-year-round driver gets, so probably he spent the spring and summer working in the woods. Logging maybe, by the look of him.

I said: "The barbotte joint a few miles out."

"Okay. They won't be open for another couple hours."

"How do you know?"

"Used to get twenty a week to tout for them. Didn't like it. I gave it up." He looked at me from the corner of his eye and apparently approved of what he saw. "If you win anything tonight, don't let them send you home in one of their own cars or you may not make it. And don't try complaining to the cops because those guys are too well protected. Maybe they'll even work up a case against you."

"They'd get disagreeable if they knew you talked like this."

"You're not the type to tell them, chum."

"Nor the type to play barbotte. This is a social call. I'll want you to wait down the road for me."

He got a shade jumpy. "Trouble?"

"What do you care so long as you keep the meter running?"

"I don't." He shrugged amiably. "But you pay me something on account before you go in."

He was a good type. We drove through the frozen countryside, talking about the cold weather and his five children, all boys. He said it was his ambition to equal his father who had fourteen. He thought the weather might help him in this because all the while the temperature stayed below zero he spent the majority of his non-working hours in bed. I wished him luck in the venture. I wished his wife luck because I figured she needed more. He thought that was very funny and was still laughing when we turned off the highway and into the side road. He killed the headlights and taxied to within a hundred yards of the driveway. He seemed reliable enough. He wouldn't go away. I gave him ten bucks and got out and started to walk.

I went through the gates and up the drive and past the trees. I didn't bother to walk on the balls of my feet because I was keeping well to the side and the snow muffled all sound except for an occasional grinding squeak. It was breathlessly cold. Two or three of the trees had frozen at the sap and burst open.

A solitary light was gleaming bright from an upper window. The ground floor was in darkness except at the back where another window shone out onto a clump of ice-encrusted bushes: maybe the doorkeeper and his wife having an evening meal, stoking up for business. If what the cabbie said was true, the croupiers wouldn't be here for at least another half hour. I turned the handle of the front door and pushed.

It was locked, an old-fashioned up-and-down lock that matched the rest of the house. I pulled out my penknife and my souvenir button-hook and went to work, praying the bolts on the other side were not drawn. I fiddled and twisted, working fast, and when the click came it sounded like an explosion in the surrounding stillness. I stood still a while, holding my breath, with the pulse in my throat beating like a smithy. I turned the handle again and slipped inside, into the warm darkness, leaving the outer door ajar. I lifted my second favorite gun from the holster and threaded my way through the tables on tip-toe, straining my eyes against the darkness, knowing the location from my previous visit. I went on up the stairs, testing each step for creaks before I put my weight down. I was frightened.

The light was coming from Maisie's office. I sidled along the landing and stood outside the door and listened. There was a brief murmur, a tiny giggle and then silence.

I waited longer. I waited until my ears were thudding like trip-hammers and my head had begun to sing. When I could stand it no longer I took a firmer grip on the gun, turned the handle and noiselessly opened the door.

They didn't see me. They were sitting on the desk and Maisie Mackintosh had her arm around the little blonde's shoulders.

I said: "Why, hello there!"

It was as if I'd set off a firecracker. They came off their perch like a couple of well-trained acrobats. The blonde flamed a furious red, turning her face aside, and Maisie went scarlet, real scared—but not surprised. Not the way she would have looked had she been thinking I was dead.

"Me," I said, waving the gun. "In the solid flesh."

The blonde was doing a tottering backaway. Maisie sand back weakly on the desk, the panic fluttering in her eyes like a flock of birds.

"So," I said. "You knocked off a Mountie. Of all the boob tricks, making a mistake and killing a Mountie."

"You're no Mountie," she said, "you lying bastard." She was trying to lash up her flagging spirits, to build herself up by beating me down. She almost spat. "You got bounced for shagging some scummy floozie while her husband was out killing a friend of yours."

I said, "Let's concentrate on the mistakes you've made, honey. You found out about me. You figured it was okay to rub me out because no one would give a damn, not like if I was a Mountie. Ain't that hilarious! So you made a mistake and knocked off a Mountie anyway."

"You son of a bitch," she snarled, "what are you trying to fix?"

"Not me," I said, "the others. They'll be on your tail from now on, Maisie, and you know what to expect from them." I couldn't mention it too often. "Honey," I said gently, "the Royal Canadian Mounted Police."

The panic came back, and big. But she wasn't questioning me, which meant she'd already known who'd been killed in my place. The leak at Headquarters again. The Syndicate had long arms and hands full of cash.

She said faintly, "You've got it wrong. I didn't have a thing to do with it."

"I believe you," I said. "The tough job is convincing the rest of the boys. Looks like the rap for you, Maisiee, unless maybe you turn Queen's evidence. Tell be about it. Could be I might help you for personal reasons."

Her face had no color. The little blonde was still standing stiff and unmoving, and suddenly a funny little moaning noise came out of her throat. Maisie didn't even look at her, but the sound seemed to crumble the last of her strength.

"What do you want me to talk about?" she said, almost whispering.

"Start by filling in the gaps about Gerald Astley."

She hesitated. She moistened her lips. She looked over now at the motionless blonde, and her great flabby face went almost pathetic, almost womanly. I saw her decision coming. "Okay," she said, "but I didn't have anything to do with the killing, I swear it. It was Charlie, Charlie Hedges. The snowbird with the knife, the one who was here last night."

"I knew that," I told her. "I want to know why. Why did I have to be gotten rid of so suddenly? What's the connection with the Romilly Club?"

She was eager now, sort of relieved, talking louder. "Your redheaded pal. He was onto something, something big. He's been living in clover this past four or five months."

She froze, and so did I. Someone was tapping very lightly on the door.

"Who?" I whispered.

She shook her head, nearly green with sudden fear.

"Okay, open the door a little way and talk natural. The gun'll be trained on your back."

The little blonde was huddling in a corner, blue eyes gone dozier than ever. I concentrated on Maisie. She walked stiffly across the room and opened the door about a foot.

"Hello," she said, and it didn't sound natural at all.

She said nothing else and the person outside said nothing. I waited for ninety or a hundred years until something cracked very loud in the silence, and I realised it was the squeaking step at the bottom of the stairs. The front door slammed.

I went forward cautiously and stood tight against Maisie's back. "Okay," I said.

She didn't move.

I took hold of the door edge and jerked it open. Her tight-clenched hand came away from the doorknob. I went to heave her out of the way and she began to fall—slowly, like a tree. She keeled right over and the back of her head went bang on the floor. She stretched out there full-length, very tall and very still and very dead. Out of her left breast was growing a long shiny bone-handled knife that I'd seen before. Little Charlie Hedges hadn't liked her talking about murder.

And then it was that the little blonde started to scream. She hurtled across the room and flung herself on Maisie's body, howling like a demented hyena. It made me nervous. Too many people were looking for me and I didn't want to attract attention. I said, "Shut up, babe," and downstairs a door banged and the lights went on in the main room. Someone was coming up.

The blonde was still at it. I reached down and yanked her to her feet. Her face was all bloody. Her eyes were rolling up with hysteria. I started to shake her, feeling sorry for her, and she went right on screeching. I drew back and let her have a fairly hefty one alongside the jaw. She went out like a candle.

"For the love of God, Maisie, I've told you before." The voice was calling from the bottom of the stairs in French and in a bad temper. "Why don't you and your girl friend be quiet?"

I emerged onto the landing and the doorkeeper was halfway up the stairs. I said, "Back up, Papa, I'm leaving," and started down medium slow. The gun was in my hand and the little blonde was over my shoulder. She was still out.

He was crafty. He looked at the gun and at her and then he grinned. "Have it here," he said. "Give her to me after. I don't care."

He made me sick. I said, "You'll care, Papa. Your boss is upstairs with six inches of steel in her teton. The police'll have to come this time. Awkward for you, eh?"

"And for you," he said, still grinning. "The Syndicate will be angry." He stopped backing up, and his eyes were flickering. He looked tricky and I hadn't the time. I lashed out one foot and kicked him in the chest, and he finished the journey downstairs like a sack of coal, groaning. He was pretty old. I jumped over him and ran for the door. The kid on my shoulder was beginning to stir. I went down the drive like a hare and out through the gates. The cabbie was sitting behind the wheel placidly smoking a cigarette.

He could move. I dumped the girl in the back and fell in after her. I didn't say a word, but he meshed his gears and we jumped forward, doing fifty almost form scratch. I waited till I got my breath back. "Listen," I said, "this kid'll start screaming when she wakes up. She's the excitable type. Don't worry."

He looked over his shoulder and his teeth flashed.

"Funny thing, my wife used to be excitable when we got married. Know how I cured her?"

"Sure," I said. "Watch the road and slow down a little."

I lifted the blonde out of the corner and made her comfortable against my shoulder. I tried to wipe her bloody little face with spit and a handkerchief. Her eyelids fluttered. She stirred and gave a subdued moan, and then her eyes widened and she got a good look at me. She opened her mouth to scream and I pressed down her lips till I could feel her even little teeth against my mouth. She fought for about twenty seconds and then the thaw set in. She melted like hot ice-cream and came back at me with the power of a new Hoover. I put a hand under each shoulder and lifted her up and sat her across my lap. The cabbie changed the angle of his driving mirror and began to whistle a loud French march.

She was a different girl when we reached the outskirts of Montreal. She was snuggling up to me and wanting more, talking to me in a piping little voice like a choirboy's.

She said she had known Maisie eight weeks and her name was Felicity Magworth and she never hoped to go back home to Three Rivers because she wanted to come home with me. I said there were certain difficulties and wouldn't she like to stay with a friend of mine whose name was Tessie. She said for sure she would so long as I paid her regular visits. I promised to do just that.

I gave Tessie's address to the driver, who was having a huge time of it. Then I had him drop me at my own address and gave him another fifteen bucks and told him to deliver the kid to Tessie and say I sent her. He said he would, and this was the best time he'd had in months.

Felicity Magworth climbed out of the back and got in front with him. She was smiling—inspired by the novelty of it all. I stood back and tipped my hat. The driver didn't take time to look at me. He did his trick with the clutch and went off down the street like a new-shot arrow. I knew the alley he was heading for and wished him luck. He was a good type, and what with five kids already he deserved any change he could get.

I went into the flat to call Tessie.

# 13

Miss Lindsay heard my key in the lock and came skittering down the passage clucking her tongue. "There's a young lady been waiting in your room more than an hour. Where were you at? A very nice young lady. She must be fed up with it by now."

"She can go any time," I said. I went throughto the Lindsay's sitting room and picked up the phone.

It's the only phone in the flat. I use the number on my business cards but it's listed in the book under the Lindsay's name, so it's in her sitting room. A good arrangement. It prevents me being pestered in my spare time by people I don't want to talk to. I dialled Tessie's number. Lindsay was hovering in the kitchen, well within earshot. Tessie's sexy purr came from the other end.

"Hello, honey," I said. "It's me. Look, there'll be a girl arriving at your place in about an hour, maybe less. Look after her. She's been a mason's mate but the mason recently croaked. She may revert to type and make passes at you. Take no notice. Her name's Felicity Magworth."

"Felicity what?" she asked. "Is that possible? What's the interest?"

"Platonic," I said. "Purely. I feel sorry for her."

"That'll be the day!" Tessie sounded acid.

"Also when she comes to her senses I might get information from her."

"Okay." Now she sounded grudging. "Okay if you say so, but I'm jealous. Don't blame me if I claw out her eyes."

"Go ahead," I said. "And listen. Break it gently to Margueritte. Tom Littlejohn got knocked off last night."

"Oh," she said. It was only a breath. There was a long silence and she added, "Sorry I snapped at you, kid."

"That's fine," I said. "Gotta go now. There's another girl waiting for me—in my room."

She said, "You louse," and began to laugh. I hung up, dialled another number and asked for Captain Masson.

The voice spoke in broken English. "He's off duty till midnight."

I switched to French. "Then listen. There's a barbotte joint just off highway nine about fourteen miles from the city. Probably you know it well."

The voice became guarded. "Who is speaking?"

"Never mind. And don't tell me the district is under Provincial Police jurisdiction. I know it already. What you don't know is that woman's been murdered out there, up on the second floor. Sort it out between yourselves who's going to make the pinch, but better hurry."

I hung up.

The Lindsay came in from the kitchen. "Anything about the filth who did that to poor Tom?"

"Yes," I said. "I know who it was for sure. Only there's no legal evidence except the word of a woman who's dead and the corroboration of a halfwit blonde."

"Well," Miss Lindsay said, "as long as you know."

I nodded and went back up the passage to my room. Someone was playing the phonograph, the Mozart records I got as a Christmas present from a girl named Ethel who wanted to make me cultured. I pushed open the door and went in. Marian Remington was sitting in an armchair, reading one of my textbooks on the use of small arms. I was glad it wasn't her stepsister. After the bout with the blonde in the cab it would have been too much.

"Bulging with money?" I asked.

She nodded so that the sheen ran around on her hair. She looked demure and beautiful, and her clothes were a knockout, a real mink. Momentarily she made all the other girls I knew seem like tramps. If she were just a little warmer. She opened a large handbag, drew out a wad of bills and smiled. I smiled too.

"You really are the hardest man to pay money to," she said. "I rang your office five times today and went down there twice. I even waited half an hour, but you never showed up. And you didn't phone me. I thought perhaps you had discovered some niceties of conscience that were preventing your taking the job after all."

"No," I said.

She smiled. "Men are such peculiar creatures. They can never be straight-forwardly malicious like women. They can never understand us for being so."

"Stop it," I said. "You know nothing about men. Your virginity's all over you like a veil. If it weren't you mightn't be so down on your stepmother and your stepsister."

She flushed a faint pink, biting her underlip. "I'm making a fool of myself," she said. "I've read a great deal and I'm at the silly age where I believe most of what I read."

"And most of what you hear."

"If you mean about my stepmother, yes I do. But only because I love my father and don't want his heart broken. He's the most wonderful man in the world."

"He's a nice guy," I agreed. "How much cash you got there?"

She handed it over. There were two hundred and eighty bucks—forty a day for exactly a week. I said: "It may take longer than this. And then there's the question of expenses."

"I don't mind. Charge as much as you like. It's a pleasure." She became aware of how viciously she had spoken and flushed again, looking down at the ground. Am I being very vile?" she asked faintly.

"Fair to middling," I said. "What is it you have against her?"

She hesitated. "So many things. There was a chauffeur once. I made Daddy fire him on the pretense that he was unsuitable, but it was really because he was suiting my stepmother too well. Daddy didn't know, he's too trusting. And there was another man who used to come from the bank, a young fellow with dark hair. She used to be shut up in the room for hours at a time with him."

"Aren't you confusing her with your stepsister?" I asked.

"They're exactly alike," she snapped, spitting venom. "It's in the blood. My stepmother is cleverer because she's older, but I'll bet both of them said nice things to you."

"Because I'm a nice guy," I said. "Do you know why your stepmother had me at the house the other night?"

"Was it something to do with Gerald?"

I nodded. "And do you know why she gave me the bum's rush all of a sudden?"

She shook her head. "I didn't know about that. Why did she?"

"The sixty-four dollar question. I thought it might have something to do with your hiring me." I stood up. The

106

phonograph was still playing so I walked over and shut it off. "When do I start?" I asked.

"Tomorrow." She smiled at me like a little girl. "But please leave the music on. I hope you didn't mind my playing it while I waited. I was telling myself that there couldn't be much wrong with a man who had The Magic Flute in his record cabinet."

I dropped the arm back on the record. "You sure do believe all you read," I said. "I just supposed you'd be wanting to go home, now the business is over."

She sat still and said nothing. She looked faintly uncomfortable. The phonograph was going plink-plink fiddle-diddle-dee, the sounds that Mozart used to write as background for everything from murder to love triumphant.

The girl dithered a bit, then fluttered into a sort of adolescent behaviour that we don't see much of these days when kids achieve maturity at the age of twelve. She blinked her eyelids rapidly. Her blush went deep red. She looked the incarnation of innocence. It was all a very pleasing sight.

She said, in a timid voice: "I like you, Mr. Garfin."

"In that case," I said, "you'd better make it Mike. Do you like the name of Felicity Magworth?"

She looked helpless. "I don't know."

"You should," I said. "Right at this moment you owe her more than you know. I might very easily be bothering you." She didn't get it and I didn't explain. We looked at each other.

"She got to her feet, embarrassed, and laughed a little. "I'm making an awful fool of myself again aren't I? What I'm really trying to do is ask you to take me out somewhere. I lead a very quiet life, Mr. Garfin."

"Mike," I said.

"Mike," she said. "You see, I never get to go out anywhere. I seldom even want to go. But just lately I've had an urge to see these exciting places where Gerald stays until four in the morning. I was hoping you would take me to one of them after dinner last night and I could have cried when you put me into the car and packed me off home like a good little girl, and that wounded my feminine instincts."

I said: "Why me?"

This time she laughed outright. "It sounds dreadful doesn't it? As if I had designs on you. But you should see some of the other gentlemen I know; they'd faint at the sort of place I want to visit. Besides, I heard Daddy say that you're a very trustworthy young man. I'd feel safe with you."

"Those," I told her, "can be included in the series of famous last words. Okay, I'm swept off my feet. You're a nice girl. I like your face, I like your figure, and I like your forty a day. Let's go. We'll have to take a cab."

"My car is parked down the road."

I said, "Good, I always wanted to ride in a portable ballroom."

She was sparkling. She could never be really warm in the way that Tessie was, but this was a good substitute. She looked like a million dollars. We went out into the biting cold and I left the lights on inside the car, just to look at her.

She let me drive, if you call it driving. In one of those things you simply sit behind the wheel and somebody silently rolls the scenery past you. We bowled along Sherbrooke Street as far as Atwater, and I turned into St. Catherine Street West and drove slowly down. It was ten o'clock on a cold night and the street was crowded as it always seems to be at every time except between three and six-thirty in the morning.

"Watch the side-streets," I told her. "Pick the prettiest sign and we'll go in."

She opened her eyes wide. "Oh, but I've been occasionally to the nightclubs at this end of town. They're very respectable. I thought you were going to take me somewhere tough. Somewhere down east."

I speeded up until we crossed Bleury and were over

in St. Catherine East, then I slowed down again, smelling a great big rat. The crowds were just as thick here, Marian Remington looked just as innocent. Yet it wasn't the same. The neons unpeeled on either side of us. The Pickup. The Muskrat. The Frou-Frou. The Romily—prop. Jean Genet.

"Any of these places," she said. She was looking from side to side, interested. "I don't come to this end of town very often. It's quite exciting."

I turned into the side-street and pulled up. I still wasn't convinced, but my gun was keeping comfortable guard over my armpit. I decided to take a chance. "Come on, blossom," I said, getting out. She pattered happily along beside me, taking my arm. It was my left arm so there was nothing much wrong with that because I'm right-handed. I unbuttoned my topcoat and made an unobtrusive practice lunge just before we reached the entrance.

A party of four was going in. I got behind and followed them up the stairs. The band was playing a calypso, a loud one. My kidneys began to ache with memory. I looked at Marian and her eyes were sparkling. There was a burst of applause, tapering off, and we were at the top of the stairs. Jean Genet was standing in the doorway, smooth and shiny and smiling, currant eyes aglow and paunch well pointed.

He didn't flex a single face muscle. He bowed. "Good evening, mademoiselle—Monsieur Garfin. Mr. Garfin, it is good to see you again. You would care to check your coats?"

"Don't bother, Marian," I said. "In a joint like this they'd change your mink for rabbit in thirty seconds flat."

"Ha, ha, ha." Genet made like it was funny. "A joke between old friends, mademoiselle. Mr. Garfin is a great humorist. A table for two, Mr. Garfin?"

"In a corner," I said. "Near the door. Send the waiter with two double whiskies."

"A lemonade for me," Marian Remington said.

"Two double whiskies for me and a lemonade for her."

"Immediately." He jerked his head a couple of times, signalling, and I saw a waiter give the polite brush-off to a couple at the corner table. We moved in after them, Genet in the rear, washing his hands with invisible soap. "Order anything you wish, Mr. Garfin. Tonight you and the young lady are our guests."

I couldn't figure it, the service and the amiability. "Two double whiskies," I said, "and a lemonade. Now beat it."

He waddled off across the room, nodding at a few lucky customers. Marian Remington was looking at me less like a schoolgirl than a schoolteacher. "Why did you have to be so rude to him?" she asked.

I grinned. "Like he said, a joke between old friends. This the sort of place you wanted?"

"Exactly." She wrinkled her nose, cute. "Exciting, isn't it? Do you come here often?"

"Oh sure, all the time. Sometimes I join the private party upstairs."

Despite the talk, this was my first visit to the club itself. I thought it looked garish, dingy, pretty tame, the sort of place where you might even find a trick cyclist in the floor show. The crowd was tame, too, a sprinkling of sharpies but the majority looking like each other and everybody else, plain everyday joes and joesses. Maybe that's why Marian Remington found it exciting. Living up there on the mountain, she probably had little contact with the plain and every day. The rich can always discover an endless novelty in the not so rich.

The waiter brought the drinks and departed, two tumblers for me and a frosted glass for her. The whisky looked good. I said: "This is corny, but there may be a knock-out in this drink. If I feel it I'm going to draw a little safe attention by firing a gun out of that window. And if I do, get up and run and don't wait to see what happens to me."

She began to giggle. "You're simply trying to make it more thrilling for me. Let me see you drink it."

110

I poured it down. Genet had brought out the best, and it tasted as good as it looked. "Okay," I said, "you can relax."

She giggled some more.

The band had stopped again and the couples were drifting from the stamp-size floor back to their tables. There was a roll of drums and a guy in evening dress bounded on, bursting at the seams with the old phoney bonhomie which earns an emcee his bread and butter. Nightclub emcees make me puke and this one was no exception. He told a couple of stories I'd laughed at in grade-school lavatory, and then informed us we were about to see the most sensational act in the city, as according to emcees we always are. I didn't catch the name of the act. I was busy watching Marian Remington's reaction to the jokes, ready to tell her she'd asked for it if she raised so much as a peep of objection. I was also thinking of other things. I was wondering what the hell went with Genet. I was trying to figure his connection with Gerald Astley's blackmail of the Syndicate. I was wondering also where Gerald Astley was moving, or stretched. And I was keeping the door in view in case little hopheaded Charlie with the knife put in an appearance. I wanted to see him very very much. I said:

"Did your stepbrother come home last night?"

"No, that's only the second night. He'll probably take another four or five yet."

There was a second roll of drums and the band began to play circus music, off-key and burlesque. A door swung open the far side of the room and there was a tremendous burst of laughter and applause. I stretched my neck. The dwarf came rolling down between the tables, dressed in a Pierrot's costume with lots of pompoms, balancing himself on the top of a huge medicine ball. He did a couple of twists and skimmed round the corner and came to a dead stop right in the middle of the dance floor, bowing to the crowd and smiling and waving. The mob lapped it up. He looked like a seal. He gazed around the dim room until he picked out where I was stting and gave me an extra bow. Then he jumped lightly off the ball. I saw that his fantastic nose was mashed and swollen where I'd socked him. It pleased me. It made my kidneys feel especially good. I joined in the applause.

The lights went down. The little guy stood spotlighted in the center of the room. In the audience a woman shouted in a boozy voice, "Look at tall, dark and handsome," and the laughter increased. The dwarf gave her a special smiling bow. The orchestra started a soft vamp. I looked across at the lighted rectangle of the entrance and decided I was fairly safe. I sat back to watch with one eye.

After three minutes I understood perfectly why the little bastard had been able to beat me up with such a quiet relish. He would probably have done it to anyone. He must have hated the whole human race, and he had good reason. The audience rode him. They sat on their hands when he did his best tricks and cheered their heads off every time he played the funny little bad-formed dwarf. They wanted to laugh. They wanted pratfalls. They wanted to see him kick his short little legs in the air like a capsized beetle. They wanted it proved to them how much more beautiful and graceful they were than he. They let him know what they wanted by hollering names at him—Tich, Shorty, Sawn-off, Duck-ass. They demanded what they wanted and they got it, and in the process the little guy was forced to make a pretty sorry spectacle of himself. His insides must have been a mass of murderous hatred.

I looked to see if Marian Remington was enjoying it. She had her head turned away, and I guessed it would be a long time before she wanted to come again to a joint like this one. I wasn't sorry for her; she'd asked for it. But I tried to figure what had made me suspicious of her earlier on.

The dwarf knew his stuff, balancing and tumbling and feats of strength that would have hospitalized the jeering joes in the audience for months on end. An assistant brought in a set of bars and we got a series of one-hand stands that would have cracked my rib cage and given me a permanent paralysis of the pectorals. The audience didn't like it. They wanted to haw-haw. The guy dropped on all fours and ran around the ringside like a dog, snapping at the women's legs. What a success that was!

I tried to feel sorry for him. My kidneys wouldn't let me. Even when he should have looked most pathetic, when the razzing was loudest and he at his most grotesque, there was still something about the little monster that made my flesh creep. A couple of times I was tempted to join in the name-calling. He was foul.

Marian Remington said nothing. Her head stayed averted. I turned to ask her if she wanted to go now, and I was just in time to see her mouth drop wide open. Her hand came over and clutched my arm.

"Oh, Mike," she whispered, and her fingers were like a vise. "Oh, Mike, but you're the clever one. You're so very extremely clever that I don't know how to thank you. How did you know about it?"

I wondered what the hell. She was breathing very quickly. I followed the line of her vision and her stepmother, plain to see, was standing in the lighted patch of doorway. She was peering in, scanning the darkened room for someone, maybe me. She looked beautiful. From the far side of the room Genet came threading his way through the tables toward her. He was hurrying. He was nervous. I saw the white outline of his face as he turned his head to where I was sitting. I knew what was the matter. He was terrified that I'd caught sight of her.

## 14

She didn't smile when Genet came up to her, but there was no trace of surprise in her face when she greeted him.

I'd have staked my life that this wasn't their first meeting, that they already knew each other. So far as appearances went I'd have won the bet immediately. Genet took her arm and she made no expression of protest. He drew her out of sight. He drew her to the right and not the left, and that meant they were going upstairs and not down. He wasn't showing her the way out.

I said, "Do I get a bonus?"

Marian Remington was smiling like a cat with a bellyful of canaries. She nodded quickly.

"Then sit still. I'm going to see what moves."

"I'm coming with you." She pushed back her chair. "I want to catch her at it."

"Don't be a dirty bitch," I snapped. "There'll be evidence enough without any of your pure virginal gloating."

For an instant the cat became a tigress; then her expression shaded to apology. "You're right, of course, Mike. I'm sorry. It's just that I hate the damn woman. I want Daddy to get rid of her."

I left her sitting there and went across to the door, feeling neither so good nor so proud of myself. I felt dirty. Anything that smacks of a prying divorce is poison to me, and this looked like a stinker. The place didn't help. Neither did the mob. They were still bawling their funny remarks at the dwarf.

But if it were only a divorce I would consider myself lucky. I poked my head around the door. Both staircases, up and down, were deserted. On the upper floor a small bulb was screwed into the ceiling, throwing a dim light over the landing. I patted my gun and ran lightly up the stairs, two at a time, on the balls of my feet.

Something moved. Somebody said, "Whadya want?" in a tough voice, and a man stepped out of the shadows. It was Joe Starkie. He recognised me.

I always thought he was stupid. Maybe they weren't

expecting me so soon, but he wasn't holding a gun. And now he tried to do two things at once. He dove a hand at his hip pocket and at the same time tried to kick me in the groin. He was way off balance. I stepped aside and swung him a real chopper that landed just below his left ear. I felt his jaw go. He went down like a log and came up again like a rubber ball, still groping for the pocket.

It was lovely. I clamped my left hand around his gorge and banged him up against the wall. His head smacked the woodwork like a game of croquet. I hit him full strength in the belly and reached for his pocket. We were both trying to get in at once. I crooked my fingers and pulled and the pocket came clean away and the gun clunked to the floor. I pushed against his throat until my fingertips were almost touching the wall, and then I let him have it. It was a pleasure.

The Irish are not a forgiving race, the French less so. I thought of Starkie standing by while I got the hose treatment and my French-Irish ancestors came out with a rush. I had myself a time. I worked on him until his face resembled a relief map of the Andes, and he was breathing in little whistles through a small hole at the side of his mashed mouth. He was a tough little skunk. I liked that. It looked longer. My knuckles were skinned raw when I let him go.

He slumped to the floor like a filleted fish, not making a sound. But even then he wasn't right out. His hand was crawling toward the dropped gun. I kicked him in the head. He made a noise like a collapsing tire and finally lay still. I straightened up, panting, and reached for the gun under my arm. A voice behind me said softly.:

"I wouldn't do that, pal, if I were you. Turn around, pal." A muzzle jammed hard between my shoulder blades.

I judged the chances of rolling for the gun on the floor. It was no go. I turned around slowly and the big guy was pointing a nasty great colt at my throat. We stared at each other. The door was behind him.

"Okay," I said. "Let's go."

He didn't move. "You're a pretty tough baby, ain't you, pal?"

"You could easily find out, chum. Tuck that iron away."

He didn't like it. He clicked his teeth together a couple of times and looked ugly. He said, "All right, pal," and stepped back and waved the gun in the direction of the stairs. "Now beat it. Beat it."

I didn't believe it. I flatly didn't believe it. I said, "And what happens after the explosion? You stuff five thousand bucks in my jeans and holler I was robbing the safe?"

"I told you to beat it, pal," he rapped.

"But pal, I'm calling on a lady. You wouldn't want to disappoint her, would you?"

I had him in some sort of spot. I couldn't figure it. "The lady left word she don't want to be disturbed, pal," he said. "Go on, beat it!" He came forward and reached out to strongarm me. The arm dropped to his side and he backed away again. Someone else was coming up the stairs.

Her shiny hair appeared first, then her wide eyes and her lush mink coat. She stopped before she reached the top stair, and took the scene in. "Is everything all right, Mike?" she asked, blinking.

"Dandy."

The big guy spoke up. "Get your boy-friend out of here, babe, or I call the cops in two minutes. You look like a nice girl. You wouldn't like to spend a night in jail and get your name in all the papers, would you?"

He got her where she lived: the precious Remington name. Even her stepmother was included in this. She thought twice and said, "Come on, Mike. We can do it some other day, now we know where it is. Please take me home, Mike."

I still didn't believe I was going to be allowed to walk off like that. Why try to knock me off one day, and be completely indifferent the next? Indifferent? He was almost protective.

So maybe Joe Starkie hadn't been carrying a gun because they'd all been forbidden to use one on me. But why?

The big guy stayed stolid. I took a chance and turned around. Down below six people came out of the club room and one of the guys glanced up and saw me. The people were fooling with their coats. The big guy couldn't do it now, even if he wanted. I took Marian Remington's arm and walked down the first flight of stairs. I got mixed up with the others and the eight of us went down the second flight in a herd, out into the biting air. I got hold of her arm again and hurried her round to the car. I slid behind the wheel. She was looking at me with a calculating eye.

"Where now?"

"Home," I said.

She gave a frown of protest. "Oh, but when I said about coming back some other day I was only fooling. That big man won't stay there all the time. I thought we could go somewhere else until he's gone away and then go back and catch them unawares. Or we could sit here and wait."

I let in the clutch and backed into St. Catherine Street. "Honey," I said, "we're going home."

She beat her hands together impatiently, petulantly. "Are you afraid that it will curtail your forty dollars a day if the job is finished too soon? I've promised you a bonus, haven't I? Don't you realise that my stepmother is up there making a mock of my father's name by committing adultery?"

"In a pigs interior," I said.

"I beg your pardon?"

I said: "The day a woman like your stepmother commits adultery with a type like Genet, I'll eat my own whatsit."

"There's no need to be coarse."

"Honey," I said, "to really appreciate coarseness you should have got a look at yourself when you were hoping to catch your stepmother."

"You're being damned rude," she snapped.

I said, "Nuts."

We drove in silence as far as Bleury. She drew away from me, way over in the corner seat, indulging in some haughty form of sulking. I couldn't have cared less. I was trying to figure the thing out, and the deeper I got the more confusing it became. Yesterday they wanted to kill me. They made a mistake and killed someone else, and now they were no longer interested. Tom had been on a narcotics case and had been indirectly killed with narcotics. Yet as far as I could see, the only connection with dope was that the killer was a snow.

It was getting crazier. Gerald Astley's mother hires me to look out for him. I go gambling with him and get beaten up as a result. Then she fires me. Next thing, she turns up and pals around with the people who gave me the works. Meantime her son was missing.

I had to think that one over twice. She had hired me more or less to protect him. If she was really mixed up with these hoodlums, then in effect she had hired me to protect her son against herself. Sure enough, good and crazy. Crazy enough for Tom and Maisie Mackintosh to get knocked off. And meantime this chilly infant next to me had tried to tie it all up with a lot babbling nonsense about adultery. It smelled, and it smelled wrong. The only straightforward thing about the case was the stepsister Geraldine. At least there couldn't be two schools of thought about what she was after. Or could there? I began to whistle softly through my teeth.

Marian Remington suddenly moved over and sat nearer. The light changed and we crossed the intersection. She put a hand on my arm. "I got angry just now," she said. "I'm sorry, Mike."

"Forget it."

She hesitated. "You claim that what I say about adultery is ridiculous. Then what is my stepmother mixed up in? What is she doing in a place like that if it's not to meet a lover?"

"I don't know," I said. "And what's all this lover business.

Stop being so darned Victorian."

She withdrew the hand. Her voice went sharper and a shade higher. "I'm paying you forty dollars a day. It's up to you to go back to that place and find out exactly what is going on."

"Is that an order?" I asked.

"Yes!" she snapped. "Turn around and go back."

"Belt up," I said coldly. "You're making my pimples bleed."

Her mountainside residence authority was outraged. She was looking at me in a fury of contempt. "I know what's the matter with you. You're afraid, aren't you? You're afraid to go back there."

"You're damn right I am," I said. "There's too much bloody malarkey in the set-up at the Romily. Next time I go back, they might change their minds again and decide to put me through a mincer. I'll wait until things clarify a little."

"You dirty contemptible coward," she said icily. "You craven wretch. I thought I'd hired a man, and now I find myself firing a weakling. You're fired. I never want to see you again."

"You'll miss the Mozart."

"Don't try to be funny. You're fired. You may keep the money since that's all you seem to be interested in."

"Fine," I said. I drew over to the curb and pulled up. "So long, honey, and it's been nice knowing you." I opened the door and put out a foot. "I'll take a cab the rest of the way home."

"Mike." Her hand came out and clutched my coat. She had changed completely, almost pleading, her eyes gone soft. "God, Mike, I don't know what's the matter with me. I'm sorry. I don't know what I'm doing. I get so mad when I think of my stepmother that I don't even know what I'm saying. Forgive me, Mike. Let's go somewhere quiet and have a cup of coffee and talk it over. I'll phone home and tell them

I'll be late and after that we'll go for a drive somewhere, out in the country, or up the mountain to the Look-Out. We can watch the lights of the city. I haven't done that in ages."

"Nor I," I said.

She was appealing, lovely, almost warm. She was leaning forward with eyes all wide and lips parted softly. I got right out of the car and stood on the sidewalk holding the door handle. "You're a pretty girl," I said. "Some other time. And don't worry about firing me. I consider myself hired until this money runs out. All I want you to do is stay out of the way and phone me if you hear from your stepbrother. Nothing else. Don't bother me. I have to go somewhere else now. Goodby, honey."

"Mike," she said.

I slammed the door and walked away in the other direction. Behind me the car started up. I looked over my shoulder and saw her drive away—steering the Cadillac carefully through the traffic. I let her get out of sight and gave her a three minutes start and then I flagged a cab.

I told the man to drive me home. It suddenly seemed that I'd had a long, hard day. I wanted some sleep.

## 15

I put the bottle away, took it out again, and poured myself a long drink. It was two in the morning and I'd been drinking since I got home. I wasn't getting high, I was getting irritable. I couldn't sleep. I was playing some more Mozart, which didn't help any. I went over to the phonograph and pulled off the disc and threw it to the ground. It was a long-player and unbreakable. For some reason that knobbed me up even more.

My mind was going over and over, churning the events

of the past forty-eight hours and trying to turn them into sense. A good investigator, they say, has everything at his fingertips. I had nothing at mine except the dirt under my fingernails. I was bollixed, and completely. I didn't like it.

I sat down and made a list of all the people connected with the case. I tried to fake up a perspective, some sort of line of reasoning, by remembering everything they'd said and done. No dice. On the one hand I seemed to be mixed up in nothing more complicated than an unsavory divorce case, instigated by a coldly malicious little bitch who was probably in love with her own father, whether she knew it or not: on the other hand—What? A guy had been swimming in gravy because apparently he was in a position to blackmail the Quebec Crime Syndicate. He had disappeared. Then someone had tried to murder me. But tonight when the golden opportunity offered itself, one of the supposed would-be murderers had chosen to play patty-cake with me.

What the hell! The situation was so outlandish I couldn't even think of any questions to ask myself. The only solution was either to find the Crime Syndicate of find Gerald Astley, both of which propositions were equally impossible. The Syndicate was probably the most subtle organisation of its type in North America, tentacles reaching anywhere and everywhere, and with pressure all the way. Uncovering it would be like trying to mine for gold at the bottom of the Atlantic Ocean. As for Gerald Astley—well, I wouldn't find him for the simple reason that I was completely convinced he was dead.

Or was I? I thought about it and didn't know any more. None of his family was worried about him, so far as I could see. Come to that, I wasn't sure he was even missing. I had only the word of his stepsister that he had been away the past two nights, and there was every possibility that she might be playing a game more devious than shagging up her stepmother. My head was aching.

I finished the drink and didn't want any more. My mouth had that chalky feeling, like the inside of a limekiln, that comes when I take alcohol without getting a lift from it. I put away the bottle and decided to go to the kitchen to make myself some coffee. I opened the door and went into the passage, and in the Lindsay's sitting room the phone bell began to ring. Before it could make it a second time I had the receiver off the hook.

"Hello."

The voice was quiet, little more than a dry whimper, like the rustling of leaves. "I want to speak to a Mr. Garfin."

"Speaking," I said.

"This is Phillip Hughes. I was talking to you earlier this evening."

"Sure," I said. I'd placed the voice. "Did you have a good time with four bucks? Doesn't go far these days, does it?" I made it casual, but I'd begun to shake inside with excitement.

"No jokes," he said, and I realised his voice was not only quie but scared. "I'm in a box at the east end of Craig Street. I'm in a bad way, Garfin. I need some more cash. Did you change your mind about doing business with me?"

"Yeah," I said. "I thought it over. Climb in a cab and come out to my place. We'll have a chat about Gerald Astley. Maybe we can come to an agreement."

I hear him take a deep breath. "There's one thing, Garfin. I think I'm being followed. Sure it's been like that before. Sometimes the trees follow me. But they change their appearance, and this little guy always stays the same. If it's your idea, I don't like it."

"Forget it," I said. "Get out here quick. Be careful. Flag the first cab."

He started to talk. He started to say something about not having any money for a cab. I didn't catch the last words. I heard a faint squeak that sounded like the door of the booth being opened, and he turned away from the mouthpiece. Then he sighed. He sighed like he didn't care anymore—like he couldn't care anymore. The phone went dead.

I was really shaking now. I shouted into the mouthpiece a couple of times and then I knew the uselessness of it. I depressed the receiver hook and dialled another number, almost breaking a finger in the hurry. They put me straight through to Masson.

"So it's you," he growled. "My friend, you are in the merde. The boys didn't like the joke about the barbotte murder you played on them this evening. The man at the board recognised your voice."

"Listen," I said. "Listen carefully. Somewhere east on Craig, right at this moment, there's a man walking or probably running or maybe even riding, who's just killed or maimed another guy in a phone booth. I think killed, most likely."

"You're drunk, Mike."

"He answers one of two descriptions. Either he's around five-ten, twenty years old, big-built and redheaded, or he's five-feet-six, slender, dark, a sallow complexion about forty-two, and wearing a large fedora hat. Send some cars down there right away." And suddenly I thought: Five-feet-six and slender. Sure. Now I remembered. The guy who went into the Remington house the night I waited for Gerald Astley outside in the car. Charlie Hedges, of course.

Masson said: "Nice of you to give us a choice, Mike, but we don't think your jokes are funny anymore. First you pick on the Provincial Police by getting them to collect a body that isn't there. Now you want to fix the City boys by sending them on a wild goose chase. We know you don't like policemen, but you'll have to do better than that. You're getting old and feeble, Mike. Drinking too much. Stay out of trouble."

He sounded as if he was going to hang up. I got frantic. "Listen, you lame-brained bastard," I said, low and vicious, "this is the guy that knocked off the Mountie last night. If a body is found in that booth and you haven't sent anybody, I'll give such a personal interview to every paper in town that you'll be pounding a bear in the suburbs within a month."

"Now your jokes," he said, "are getting tasteless." But he was sounding uncertain.

I said: "Listen. If you love that great wife of yours as much as I do, send three or four cars down there right away."

I got him. I heard him murmur something to someone in the room with him. Then he said, "Repeat those descriptions."

I gave them to him, fast. I said: "If it's the little guy then probably he'll be coked up to the eyes. I don't think he's carrying a gun or he'd have killed me earlier this evening, but there's maybe a knife and he's handy with it."

I waited while some voices mumbled and a lot of feet went pounding. Masson came back to the phone. His voice was calm and measured.

"Look, Mike," he said, "we've been good friends a couple of years. I like you and my wife likes you. If I had any children they'd like you, too. But if this is your idea of funny humor and I'm left holding the sack, I'm going to make it a full time occupation to destroy you. Get down here as soon as you can. I want you under my hands when the boys get back."

He hung up.

I went down to the Lindsay's bedroom, knocked and entered. She was sitting up in bed, reading the inevitable book. I figure she'll be doing the same thing on Judgement Day, and they'll have to send out a special posse of angels to look for her. And Sir Walter Scott will be snuggling up to her just the same.

"Did you hear me come in this evening?" I asked.

She nodded. "You were early. I like the music you've been playing."

"Good," I said. "I might need the alibi. Just in case a

bunch of angry cops try to hang a murder on me, in a fit of pique. I'm going out now. I'll try not to kick over the milk bottles."

She turned her head so that she was looking at me directly. The reading lamp showed up the traces of tears on her face. I could see she'd had a bad day over Tom. "Look after yourself," she said, and the tears came again, filling her old eyes and brimming over. She picked up her book and turned a page. "That poor lad," she said. "That poor, poor laddie. Now go away and leave me with Sir Walter."

"I'll be at the police station," I said. "Don't worry, there's nowhere safer." She sniffed once more as I went out and closed the door.

The night was sheathed in cold, stark and brittle. The neons chittered through the clear air with abnormal brightness, gaudy and nasty, casting a blood-red reflection on the trampled snow. The cab driver looked tired. The city looked gimcrack. There was a foul taste in my mouth and a scooped away feeling in my belly. I was suddenly sick and frightened, like the time years ago when I came out of school late and found all the other kids had gone home and left me alone.

And I hit rock bottom. Sure. I was alone. Me. Tough private eye. Big-time operator. Six-one, a hundred-and-ninety pounds and almost thirty, sitting in the back of a cab and feeling I wanted to bawl, just because murder had come too near to home and I had known some of the blood that splashed me. Just because people were tricky and crafty and ruthlessly on the grab, and any one of them could enlist my help for a few lousy bucks a day. Just because being a private eye is not a noble profession, and because I'd once been a Mountie. Something like that. Something to do with the black canyons of modern cities, the jungles of brick where the cannibalistic human animal comports with a ferocity that would shame the beasts. Something like that. I had it bad. I wanted sympathy. I said to the driver:

"What do you think of people?"

He lowered his lids over jaundiced eyes. "Mister," he said, "I hate their goddam guts."

That made me feel better. I gave him a two buck tip which made him feel better. I got out of the cab and crossed the sidewalk quite sprightly, prepared to do battle. I went into the police station.

"Captain Masson's waiting for you."

Only the sergeant spoke. I figured they'd elected him beforehand. The rest stared. I said, "Don't you guys have anything to do?" and passed along the passage, followed by a battery of cold eyes. The place smelled, as cop shops always do: ink, uniforms, carbolic, polish, the odor of hired virtue. I still wasn't feeling good, but better now than in the cab. I needed some antagonism to put the Irish back in me.

I knocked on Masson's door and walked in without waiting for shouted permission. He was sitting behind his desk, puffing nervously on a pipe and looking haggard. There was another man with him. It was Frankisson. I got nervous myself.

I always try to like an honest cop, but with Frankisson I fail. The thing I like least about him is his rank. It's too high. The next thing is his long thin face—those loving eyes, just like a barracuda's. There's not a spark in them that could remotely be called human. He's cold, passionless, and completely automatic. His incorruptible honesty has sat on him so long and hard that it's almost a vice. He never deviates by a hairbreadth. So far as he is concerned there is no God but the Law—and Frankisson is its prophet. And heaven help the heretic foolhardy enough to question one word of the Law's divine utterances. The prophet Frankisson will descend on the offender with a sword of flame. Or with a beating-up with wet towels. Or with that delicate treatment—a Canadian favorite—where they put your feet in and out of icewater until you howl for mercy. When Frankisson is convinced of a man's guilt he stops at nothing to get the confession. And Frankisson is seldom wrong. There is one recorded mistake that he made, but he was so honestly contrite about it that the victim never pressed charges. Also, Frankisson paid all the hospital bills out of his own pocket and, the rumor goes, made the guy a peace offering of five thousand.

He'd never pay me five thousand, that was for sure. The law was the law and private investigators were just vermin on the body of the law. I hoped I wasn't due to be his second recorded mistake. The look on his face didn't much encourage me.

He pinched his razor edged nose and looked at me over the fingers. "Is this the man?" he grated.

He knew damn well I was—and who I was. This was all part of the treatment—impersonal, academic. Masson cleared his throat. "Yes, sir, it is."

Frankisson nudged a chair with the toe of his shoe. "Sit down here Mr. uh Garfin. Make yourself comfortable. There are several things I wish to ask you."

I ignored him. I said to Masson: "Any word yet from the radio boys?"

Masson was shaking his head, opening his mouth to speak, but Frankisson cut in with a voice like a fall of gravel. "I ask the questions here, Mr. Garfin. You and I are going to have a long talk with each other. You are going to explain some things to me."

"Shall we go through to the radio room?" I asked Masson.

Frankisson's fist came smashing down on the desk. He stalked across the room, yanked open the door and yelled down the passage, "Under no circumstances are we to be disturbed." Then he stamped back and confronted me with his lifeless fish-eye stare.

He hadn't really lost his temper. He was incapable of anything so human. This was all part of a calculated method he perfected years ago, when he'd found it the best way to frighten poor gibbering joes who'd been caught shoplifting. With me it didn't work. I yawned.

"Tired, Mr. Garfin?"

"You know how it is. An exhausting day."

"So I understand," he said. "You start by deceiving the Force about the identity of a corpse. You continue by tricking one of our doctors into making a false report. You inform the Provincial Police, through us, of a second murder that has not been committed, and you supply a grand finale by sending six of our cars chasing around Craig Street. A very busy day I should say, but we don't like it, Mr. Garfin. We want to know your reasons."

"I'm glad you sent six cars," I said. "The guy you're after is a tricky bastard, whichever of the two he turns out to be. He killed Tom Littlejohn. He also committed the murder that wasn't committed—a woman called Maisie Mackintosh. But I'm not surprised the boys didn't find the body. In fact I'm astonished they even found the place. It's a barbotte joint, and barbotte joints are against the law. The law around here doesn't usually like to find anything that's against the law, does it?"

Frankisson's mouth went tight, his face more expressionless. He knew about the barbotte joint and how it was kept open, and if it had been in his jurisdiction he'd have closed it down in two seconds, whatever the pressure. But he didn't like me talking that way about cops, any cops. The Law was God, he was the prophet, and the police—down to the greenest rookie—were the priesthood. As such, and no matter what they did, they were above criticism. Particularly from scurvy civilians who were also private eyes. He looked at me frigidly.

"Your motives, Garfin?"

"Wait," I told him, "until they pick up the guy on Craig. He'll explain things for you. There's a couple of questions I want to ask him myself."

The barracuda eyes showed the fish was about to attack. Frankisson spoke very quietly. "I'll give you two minutes. If by that time you haven't started talking, I'm going to book you."

"On what charge?"

He twisted his mouth, a bleak little smile. "It's a cold night, Garfin, for anyone to walk around barefooted."

"Or to be massaged with wet towels."

"Quite so."

"I belong to an ethical profession," I said. "I have a client who's entitled to remain anonymous. I say nothing until the guy from Craig Street gets here. If he spills anything I'll give as much corroboration as I can."

Masson knocked his pipe against the desk. "He's within his rights, sir."

"Shut up, Captain. I can get along without your advice." Somebody tapped the door and Frankisson's head reared back. "Get out!" he shouted. "We're not to be disturbed."

It was like a line from one of the books I used to read as a kid. The door opened and in walked Collis of the Mounted. He wasn't in uniform and he appeared to have just got out of bed. His nod to Frankisson was icily correct, but back of his eyes he looked eager.

I had not seen them together before. The superficial resemblances between them only made the main difference more marked. Both were cold. Both were shot through with self-discipline. Both were rigid and unflinching. But whereas one was a robot, the other was a human being. And despite his correct front, I'd never seen Collis look so human before. He turned from Frankisson and pointedly addressed Captain Masson.

"Forgive the intrusion. One of my men at headquarters was listening to the radio. He heard a call saying that the person your men have just brought in had something to do with the murder of Sergeant Littlejohn. He knew that I would naturally be interested, so he phoned me."

I stood up. "Just brought in?"

"So I understand."

Masson flipped a switch on his desk. "Sergeant Leroy back yet? Send him in."

The four of us stood motionless, listening to the feet come clumping up the passage. Frankisson looked madder than a mamba and not nearly so friendly. I wondered if maybe he'd been born in a quarry.

# 16

There are the Black Irish and, looking just like them, the Black French-Canadians. The two-hundred-and-fifty pound sergeant who appeared at the door would have looked equally at home in County Mayo. Masson glanced apologetically at Collis. "Do you mind, sir, if the sergeant speaks in French? His English is not excellent."

I liked that. It was a sort of reprisal. He'd never admit it in public, but Frankisson speaks almost no French at all. He was about to be cut right out of the picture. Collis nodded agreement and I grinned. Frankisson looked sweet as a lemon.

The sergeant came originally from somewhere in Upper Quebec and retained the accent. He sounded like a grizzly with a sore throat. He blinked owlishly around the room, not very brightly. He said:

"The man is dead, Captain."

Even Frankisson could get that much. He looked at me with cold satisfaction, then back to the sergeant. Masson was giving me something very like pity out of the corner of his eyes.

I said: "What color hair did he have?"

The sergeant, like a good sergeant, ignored the question. "We found a boy in the phone box with a knife wound in his back. He is dead also. I fanned out the cars to cover twenty blocks and we combed for either of the two men described.

The little man with the big hat was in the doorway of a pawnbroker's shop about two hundred yards away. He did not seem to want to escape. He did not even run away when we came up."

"He was flying a kite," I said.

This time I got attention. "That's correct," the sergeant agreed. "He was very happy. He had blood on the front of his coat and he was whistling a song. But we were careful. We approached with caution. We asked him what he was doing and he went on whistling. We got hold of him to put him the car to bring him here. He stopped whistling. Constable Gabin was holding his arm while I opened the door. Two of the other cars were coming down the street. The little man pulled a knife from his sleeve and stabbed Constable Gabin in the shoulder. I pulled out my gun and shot the little man in the chest. He is dead. He had two other knives on him."

"Why didn't you search him?"

"The knives were thin. We did not feel them."

"And Constable Gabin?" Masson asked.

"The doctor is attending him."

"Okay, make out a report."

The sergeant clumped off down the passage. I buttoned my coat and prepared to leave. Frankisson crossed the room, closed the door, and leaned against it.

"So the man is dead," he said softly. "I gather he told us nothing. Now comes the turn of our friend here, Mr. Garfin. Start talking, Mr. Garfin."

In a way it was a choice. In another way no choice at all. Both the Remington women had hired me to protect the family name. They were influential people. Word would get around. The papers would snatch up anything. One peep out of me and I might as well apply for a job with the city's snow-clearing gang. My days as an investigator would be over. I said:

"Me? I don't have anything to say."

Frankisson's eyes went from fish to cobra. He pinched his nose again. His mouth was a slit—and mean. Mean as muck. "We shall begin," he said, "by discussing the Mounted Policeman who was found dead this morning."

"Discussed already," I told him, "with both these gentlemen here. This morning, probably before you were out of bed."

He was in a spot. He would have liked to bring on the wet towels immediately, but it wasn't practical. Masson would have let it pass because Frankisson was his superior—he would have sat back not liking it but letting the guts be beat out of me all the same. But Collis was a different proposition. He, too, believed in the sanctity of the law, only he had different ideas of enforcing it. He would have raised hell at the idea of third degree, even practiced on someone he personally thought a crumb. And there was also the fact that the two men held high positions in totally different organisations. Each would look on the other's behavior with the cold eye of a rival. Each would be feeling the other's look, and behaving accordingly.

One thing was obvious. I had to get out of this office at the same time as Collis or my kidneys were in for an awful lot more aching. I raised a smile. "Well, good night everyone."

"One moment!" Frankisson remained jammed against the door. "There's the matter of a body the Provincial Police went seeking tonight. Perhaps you could tell us a little more about that."

"Me?"

"Yes, you. Why did you phone in?"

"Not me. I didn't make a phone call. Who said I made a phone call?"

He gritted his teeth until a lump appeared in either side of his jaw. If a mad dog had bitten him at that moment, the mad dog would have died. "Smart," he said. "Very smart, Garfin. Then maybe you'll enlighten us as to how you knew there'd be a body in a phone booth, down on Craig Street.

Or how you knew the identity of the little man in the fedora. In this case you were talking to a friend of yours who knew your voice. Or do you deny phoning Captain Masson?"

"Not at all," I said. "I wanted him to give my love to his wife." I looked over at Masson. "Didn't I, my friend?"

"Yes."

"And what else?" Frankisson snapped.

I dropped my voice to a deep growling bass. "I didn't know voices on telephones were accepted as legal evidence. Personally, when I make phone calls I always speak like this. It's a fad of mine. Cute, isn't it?"

Collis said: "If you gentlemen will excuse me, I'll be going."

"Me, too," I said.

Frankisson laid one finger lightly on my arm. "You're under arrest," he said.

I shrugged him off, grinning. "I've bad news for you, chum. An airtight alibi that covers me for more than two hours before the murder and sets me five miles away. Vouched for by one of the most respectable old ladies in town. And I have a licence for my gun."

"You're under arrest. The charge is loitering with intent."

I looked at Collis. "Can he do that?"

Very gently, very rigidly, very automatically, Frankisson turned the handle and opened wide the door. "I'm going to get you, Mr. Garfin," he said softly. "I, Frankisson, am personally going to get you. I won't need any help. I shall do it alone. And now get out. Get out quickly."

"Goodnight, friends," I said and tipped my hat.

I walked down the corridor, hearing Collis come behind me. I noticed how he had automatically fallen into step. I walked across the main room where the atmosphere hadn't warmed any, and out through the main door into the cold, snow-ridden night. A cab was coming by. I gave him the whistle. Collis came and stood at my shoulder and I said, "Can I give you a lift?"

He shook his head.

"For what it's worth," I said, "I'm pretty sure the guy they brought in tonight was the killer of Tom Littlejohn."

"Who was he?"

"I don't know. I figure he was a professional under hire."

"To whom?"

"I don't know."

"You should talk more, Garfin."

I said: "I talked too much already. Otherwise maybe Tom Littlejohn wouldn't be dead."

He suddenly gave me a look that was decent and good. He showed no inclination to continue the conversation. I got into the cab and he leaned forward before I could close the door. "There was nothing on your car," he said. "It was wiped clean. You can have it any time you like; it's only in our way."

He turned on his heel and walked off through the snow.

I slammed the door and sank back in the seat, ramming my hands deep in my pockets. The driver looked round with cocked eyebrows and I told him to take me to Tessie's address. Tonight was a night when I really needed a secretary.

## 17

I spent a pretty active time during what was left of the night. I fell asleep with Tessie's head on my shoulder just as the window was beginning to lighten. I guess I was tired. I didn't wake till after three. Tessie had been out to buy me a sirloin and it was the smell of cooking that woke me. I got out of bed and put on my underwear and padded out to the kitchen. She was standing over the stove wearing a frilly little apron that looked a bit silly up against her big thighs.

She was pushing back a lock of hair that kept falling over her right eye. A table was set for two and she flicked an eye over me and told me severely to go put the rest of my clothes on in case I caught cold. Her favorite theme. I did as she said. I even washed. When I returned the steak was ready.

"This will put it back into you," she said, slapping about two pounds rare on my plate. She said no more. We ate in silence.

She poured me a third cup of coffee and I lit a cigarette. She was looking at me with contracted brows. "What about the Felicity kid in there?"

"In where?"

"Marguerite took her off to an all-night party last night. They got back here around noon, still plastered. They're sleeping it off. The trouble was I told Marguerite about Tom Littlejohn and she went off to drown it in an ocean of gin. She's taking it bad."

"She'll go right on taking it bad for about a week," I said. "Then she'll be practical. There's too many men in the world for a girl like Maggie to brood over any one in particular. Besides, she's smart. She's wise to the fact that misery'll spoil her looks, and consequently her living. Show me a whore who isn't hard-headed and I'll show you an Italian that doesn't like kids."

"Say some more sweet things," Tessie said acidly. "I suppose I won't brood over you when you get knocked off. That's what's gonna happen, you know. I expect it any day now." She looked at me with suddenly widened eyes. "My God, what am I doing! I'm putting a hex on you."

"Forget it," I told her. "We've got years to go yet."

"Amen to that," she said. "But don't think you're side-tracking me away from Felicity Magworth. What d'you want me to do with her? Sign her on as an apprentice?"

"Send her home," I said, "as soon as I've seen what she knows. I'll bet my last dollar it's nothing."

"I thought you might have plans for her. Designs."

"On a child that age? Don't be ridiculous. What do you think I am?"

Tessie blew me a genteel little berry.

"There's someone else," I said, "who'll be worrying about me. Another female." I went to the phone and dialled Miss Lindsay. Her accent came through thicker than ever. She sounded agitated.

"Where've you been all night?"

"With a broad."

"Oh." I heard her sigh with relief. "That's all right then. By the way, that young lady phoned you this morning, Marian Remington. We had quite a long talk: I must say she seems very fond of you."

I was holding the phone quite tight. "What's the message?"

"She had a phone call last night soon after she got in—she said you'd know when that was—from a fellow named Phillip Hughes. He told her that her stepbrother—just a minute, I've got it all here on a piece of paper—yes, that the stepbrother, Gerald, is in Toronto and that he, this Phillip, is going up to visit him. He said he was catching a train at one-thirty and would she take some money downtown for him so he could take it to her stepbrother, who's broke. She told him it was too late at night and would he postpone going away until today. She's made him an appointment to take him some money at the Windsor Station at seven o'clock this evening. And she very much wants you to call her."

"Okay, honey," I said, "thanks. I'm going to hang up now."

"Look after yourself, dear boy." There was a click.

Tessie was looking at me with feline eyes. "For God's sake," I protested, "the woman is seventy-two."

"With you what difference would that make?"

I tch-tched her. She began to grin and called me a boar. I dialled the second number and wondered what sort of voice

136

would fool the maid. I decided to speak entirely in French. If she couldn't understand she'd at least be able to pick out the name I wanted.

"Hello?"

I hadn't expected it. It was the rich purring voice that had started all this trouble. It was Mrs. Remington. I said: "If you've fired that push-faced maid of yours, I congratulate you."

She sounded amused. "I'm afraid she's only at the back of the house. Who is this speaking, please?"

I plunged for shock tactics. I said: "If you still have the photograph of Gerald I returned to you, I suggest you tear a half of it off. The other kid, Phillip Hughes, got a knife in his back last night. Quite a mess, they tell me."

She was no longer amused. Her voice was gone dead, frozen as the weather outside. "I'm sorry, Mr. Garfin, I have no wish to speak to you."

"I noticed that at the Romily last night."

There was a long pause—so long I considered saying something else. Then: "Are you trying to blackmail me, Mr. Garfin?"

"Look," I said. "A kid's been killed. Your son is supposed to be in Toronto and he may be killed, too. If there's anything you can tell me, spill it!"

She said—quite flatly, "You're lying. I don't know what your motive is, but you're lying. If you set foot near this house of dare to phone again I shall immediately call the police. Do I make myself perfectly clear?"

She sounded as if she were keeping her voice like that to disguise the fact she was frightened. I said, "Hooey! You wouldn't dare call the police and have that impeccable Remington name all smirched up with—"

It was as far as I got. She hung up on me. I stood up and saw that Tessie was regarding me curiously. "You in trouble?" she asked brightly. "Come and tell your old Aunt Tessie all about it."

Between Tessie and the Lindsay, it seems I spend my life being asked by women if I'm in trouble. "Forget it," I said. "Nuts. I'm fine."

She came over and pushed me into a chair and settled on my lap. "You look fine to me anyway," she said.

I was figuring things out. It had been around six the previous evening when Snowy Etheridge entered the restaurant. The waitress had served him within two minutes, which meant he was probably a regular. If he was on time tonight I could still shoot up to Windsor Station by seven o'clock in case somebody else came to collect the money from the Remington girl—provided the Remington girl wasn't lying. I looked at the clock. There were two hours to go. I said to Tessie, "Honey, what can we do to pass the next two hours?"

She grinned. "Well, for one thing, I could cook you another sirloin."

"That sounds fine," I said, and we both grinned.

Before I left I took a look into the other bedroom. Marguerite and the young kid were still asleep and they looked cute, black hair and blonde side by side. I didn't have the heart to wake them up. I went out.

## 18

I had guessed right. Snowy Etheridge was sitting in the same dump, at the same table, slowly munching his way through a chef's salad. The same waitress was languishing at him from her position by the counter. She scowled when she saw me. I wondered how anyone so presumably smart as Snowy could always sit so far as a belief in his own eternal good luck. I sat down in the chair opposite him and waved off the waitress with a hand. Snowy went right on munching.

"Expecting anyone again?" I asked.

"Just you."

"Then we've probably made the same deductions," I said. "I talked to a cokie kid and nobody saw me except your pal. Your pal afterwards talks to you. You know where they're selling it these days so you comb the joints. Maybe you find the kid, maybe you don't; it doesn't matter. But somehow you get a nugget of information, a list of his connections, a line on what he probably knows, and you put them all together, knit one and purl two, and decide to peddle it. Who to?"

Snowy speared a piece of tomato with his fork and looked injured. "Mike. You got me wrong, Mike. I wouldn't peddle anything."

"You'd peddle your own tail," I said, "if you could get a customer. Cough up."

"Don't speak so rough, Mike," he entreated, chewing gently. "It's taking the edge off my appetite."

"The kid you fingered yesterday doesn't have an appetite any more," I said. "They knocked him off last night."

"Aah." He swallowed and took a deep breath. His eyes kindled with obvious interest. "Knocked off, eh?" he murmured thoughtfully. "I didn't know about that. It puts another complexion on the matter, puts the prices up, if you follow my meaning. What do you wanna know, Mike?"

"The connection between the Romilly Club and the barbotte joint out on Highway Nine. What they got in common besides making suckers of the public?"

He laid down his fork. His eyes gave two flicks that took in the room and all its occupants. "Not here, Mike," he said. "Something less complicated, something that takes less time to tell. And mention a price."

"Okay, here's an easy one. Who and what is Mrs. Remington, formerly Mrs. Astley, visitor at the Romilly, friend of Genet, and mother of Gerald Astley whose pal you put the finger on last night?"

He wiped his mouth, starting to talk while the napkin

was still in front of his face. "You're getting tougher, Mike. You're wanting me to dig up the roots. Let's get out of here. And you'd better start thinking about money. This one is gonna cost."

He stood up and took a deuce and a one from his pocket. He tucked them under the plate and nodded across at the waitress who looked as if she was about to swoon. He went over to the rack, followed by the eyes of nearly every woman in the place, shrugged his way into an alpacama that made him look all shoulders and no waist, placed a snap brim beaver fedora on his crisp chestnut curls, and gave a final twiddle of his fingers to the adoring waitress. He went out through the door.

After the Lord Mayor's show, they say, comes the manure cart. I followed after him and I was an anti-climax. The eyes dropped away from me with a listless lack of interest. But at least, I told myself, I have my honor, and that made me grin. I had damn all else.

He was waiting for me out on the sidewalk. "I have an apartment over this place," he said. "Let's go up where we can talk. I might even give you a drink."

The restaurant was on a corner. He led the way round to the narrow side street and through a small door, painted green. The place smelled vaguely of boiled cabbage, and the narrow flight of stairs we went up were crummy and unswept. I let him go three steps ahead, just in case. I knew he wasn't carrying a gun because I'd studied his beautifully tailored clothes in the restaurant and there was no bulge, but for safety I put in a hand and loosened my gun in its holster. Snowy was not notorious for rough play, and I doubted he'd ever heard a gun fired in anger, but he might have friends up there. I stood well back while he fiddled with the key and pushed the door open.

He switched on the light right away and I got down off my toes. The apartment had two rooms and the communicating door was open. There was no one else in sight.

More important, I couldn't feel anybody else about. I went in and shut the door behind me.

The place was a surprise. Snowy had taste. Gibbons furniture counteracted by walls hung sparingly with Van Gogh and Matisse. Everything was imitation, but good imitation and expensive. Information peddling obviously paid a lot more than private investigation. Snowy took off his coat and hat and dropped them onto a sofa. I sat in the only armchair in the room, which happened to be in front of the liquor cabinet. The decanters might have been Lalique, but were probably imitations, too. Anyway they were full. I said:

"Let's chat, Snowy."

Yeah, okay, it was stupid of me. I should have known. Snowy was too old a hand to let his eyes light up like in the restaurant, unless he really wanted them to. And he was being a little too offhand about the money question, for the stingy sort of bastard he was. I should have moved when he moved. I sat there like a cretin.

He said, "We'll have a drink first," and moved behind me to the liquor cabinet. The blackjack may have been lying in full view or it may have been hidden behind the decanters. I don't know. It came down on me and my head exploded. I pitched forward with the red whorls gyrating in front of my eyes like Catherine wheels. I rolled over on my back and put the palms of my hands on the carpet, trying to push myself up. I saw for the first time that the ceiling was papered in alternating little squares of white and silver, and they were dancing, forming a background for Snowy's looming shape. Everything was slowed up. I pushed hard with my hands and nothing happened. Snowy was getting larger and larger, moving like a high-jump man in a slow-motion newsreel. He sank gracefully onto one knee beside me and he was smiling an enormous smile. He lifted the blackjack again and I tried to say, "Don't, Snowy," and I tried to move, but nothing happened. The black thing curved down through the air and hit me square on top of the forehead, just above the hair line. I heard myself groaning, and then I went down into the dark.

# 19

It was a long, long time. I thought I heard voices and then it seemed that someone was putting me to bed. But the voices went away again. I was alone in the dark. I thought I was back in the Mounted Police and up in the Barren Lands until suddenly the scenery changed and I was standing at the corner of Peel and Windsor, directing traffic. I held up a large Cadillac to let a man cross the road. He had a fat smooth face and a pointed paunch, but only when he'd got out of sight did I realise it was Genet. Then I looked at the clock and it was almost seven and I knew he was going to Windsor Station to meet Marian Remington. I started to run because I had to warn her, and somewhere a band struck up a calypso. I heard the traffic honking. But no matter how hard I ran I stayed in the same spot and got nowhere. Something had a hold of me and was pulling me back, back, back until I was running on the backs of my heels and my head was thrown back so that I could see nothing but the sky. The harsh blue descended and went through my eye sockets, into my head like a couple of saw-edged knives. I closed my eyes trying to shut it out, and then I opened them again and everything was white—a plain white this time, with no little squares. It rocked and swayed like the horizon from a stormbound ship.

The voices came back and began to disengage. One of them said: "Throw some more cold water on the son of a bitch."

Another replied: "I don't have time now, anyway."

I couldn't move hand or foot. Somebody had their hand in my hair, bending my neck back to an almost ninety degree angle, shaking my aching head until I thought it would come off. I said: "Okay, okay, okay," pretty frantically, and the hand let go. I kept my neck like that, not wanting to move for a few seconds, wishing I could slip back into consciousness, now that I knew where I was.

The overhead white teetered into position. It was the whiteness of the whitewashed ceiling in the apartment over the Romily Club. I saw the etching on the wall, the black and white color scheme. I was tied to a chair with a thoroughness that indicated the big guy, but when I lowered my head from the position into which it had been jerked the big guy was nowhere to be seen. Neither was Jean Genet. I was looking into the piggy little eyes of the dwarf and he was smiling, curving his upper lip until the tip of his fantastic nose seemed to be growing from his teeth.

"Hello, Mr. Garfin," he said sardonically. "I've got a long swingy piece of rubber pipe waiting for you."

"You've got a long swingy nose," I said.

He bunched his fist and hit me in the face and the blood splattered all ways. It didn't help my headache any. I felt myself going out again and tried to push it the whole way, but no luck. I opened my eyes again and everything was the same except that Henry Starkie was standing beside the little guy. He was smiling the smile of a serpent confronted by a young and juicy rabbit.

"Dat's good," he said. "Dat's very funny. Do it some more." He reached forward and delicately took the upper lashes of my right eyelid between his thumb and forefinger. He gave a sharp pull and I thought I'd lost my forehead. I figured I wasn't going to look so pretty when I got out of here—if I got out. He showed me the eyelashes and began throwing them on the floor one by one, saying, "He loves me, he loves me not. He loves me, he loves me not." The dwarf was convulsed. They were a very funny couple.

"I caught your act last night, Lofty," I said. "Very good. I enjoyed it."

"Yeah, I heard you were here." He smiled maliciously. "So did Starkie didn't you, Stark?" The 'he-loves-me' business had stopped and Starkie was looking at me with his eyes gone like hot currants. "One brother put in jail by you," the dwarf continued, "and the other in hospital as of last night, and now our friend Starkie feels he has to do something to redeem the family honor, don't you Stark?"

He didn't say anything. He didn't need to.

"Sorry you won't be catching my act again, tonight, Mr. Garfin. A real pity, I'm breaking in a new routine. I'll have to be gone in a couple of minutes and then you'll be all alone with our friend Starkie. But don't worry too much. He's promised to leave a piece for me, haven't you Stark?"

I said: "Why not pump me full of whatever dope is fashionable this week and then park me out in the snow. It'll save everyone a lot of trouble."

"But we love trouble, don't we Stark?" the dwarf insisted, grinning. "And we don't want to use that other routine again. It might get monotonous. No sir, Mr. Garfin, we've got a nice spot picked out for you, under the river. Very neat when you think of it. If there's anything left of you in the spring it'll be ground to hamburger when the ice breaks." He chuckled. "Course, there may not be much left of you when we put you in. Starkie and I want some fun first, don't we Stark? And the boss wants some information."

"Ask away," I said, and I couldn't keep the desperation out of my voice. "I'll tell anything you want to know."

"But I don't know what questions to ask. The boss is out on a job and won't be back for two or three hours. No,"—the dwarf shook his head regretfully—"I'm afraid you're gonna have to be left alone with Starkie. It won't be so bad."

I had to keep talking. I had to postpone whatever games they intended to play before putting me under the ice. "There's blood on your shirt," I told the dwarf.

"From your nose this time, Mr. Garfin. Tit for tat. Life's

like that."

"Dat's poetry," Starkie said.

"And he hit your brother on the nose yesterday," I said. "With a rubber pipe. Don't forget that."

Starkie scowled and leaned forward. I thought he was going to pick more eyelashes. "Lofty said he was sorry and me brudder said it was okay," he said. "It was you what done the damage." He lifted a hand and patted me gently on the head. It was more menacing than if he hit me hard. It promised things to come.

I looked around, sizing my chances of escape. The door to the stairs and the door to the adjoining room were firmly closed. The window was thickly draped. I tried some practice pressure on the ropes and gave up the idea of escape, entirely. I wondered what the time was and how they'd got me here. I said:

"What did you pay Snowy for the caper?"

"Money and good words," the dwarf flipped. He was going to add something else but a voice cut across, coming from behind the closed door of the other room. It was a woman's voice and I recognised it. It called petulantly:

"What are you doing out there, Lofty? Come it and be nice to me."

Both of them jumped. Starkie's face went tight and mean. "I t'ought dat screwy tart left hours ago," he snarled. "The boss don't like it. Get her outta here."

They were no longer pals.

"Hold your horses," the dwarf sneered. "Just because you're not getting any."

"I wouldn't touch that—"

"Yeah," the dwarf interrupted, "and that's a likely story. Don't worry, I'll send her out by the back way. I got to go in and change for the show anyway."

So there was a back way.

"Don't let her see this guy," Starkie said.

"She'll keep her mouth shut." The dwarf pulled off his shirt and turned round a couple of times. He was pretending unconscious but really showing off the muscles on his back and chest. He was proud. He gave a final twist and went in, leaving the door ajar. We couldn't do anything after that but listen.

The effect on Starkie was something to see. He prowled up and down the room with a face the color of putty, then after a while he went over quietly and closed the door. Then just for the hell of it he came back across the room and hit me a roundhouse across the face with his open hand. He was in a fury, and I guess he had good reason, but he hadn't hurt me much.

I said: "I can get you a girl if you really want one."

He hit me again with the other hand, and then a quick one-two-three, using both fists. I closed my eyes and slumped forward, trying to figure a plan. I looked up from under my lids and saw him go to a cupboard and pour himself a long drink of Scotch which he sipped neat, leaning against the wall. He looked like he was raking his memory for choice things to do to me when I recovered. I stayed unconscious and he left me alone.

He was really in a bad way. He was almost pitiful to see. He had shut the door and yet he was straining his ears, trying to hear what went on in the other room. His sips got longer and ended in a gulp. He poured another Scotch.

The dwarf wasn't long. There was a long low cry that made Starkie click his teeth together and the woman began to laugh. Starkie swallowed his second drink. He was having a grim time. Even in my condition I was thinking thoughts, and Starkie was in the pink. He was shaking when he put the glass down on the sideboard. He turned quickly, savagely, when finally the dwarf came out and closed the door behind him. The little guy had got all dolled up in his pierrot's costume.

"You got rid a dat crazy bitch?"

"She'll be going. You don't have to see her." The dwarf was preening himself, purring, rubbing it in. "You been playing with junior here?"

"The son of a bitch passed out."

"Bring him round and start again. Have fun. I got to get down for the show." The dwarf crossed the room and opened the door leading to the stairs, standing on the threshold, flexing himself. "Don't you wish you had my charms?" he said. He went out.

Starkie picked up the empty glass and smashed it into a corner, then he came back and yanked savagely at my hair a couple of times, for luck. It didn't ease him any. He was calling me a running stream of inelegant names, and I heard the click of his cigarette lighter as he moved round behind me. He had to work it off somehow, and I was the handy one.

The flame licked across the knuckled of my left hand. I held it as long as I could and then I had to yell. I could smell myself. I felt sick.

"Faking, eh?" Starkie slapped my face and got hold of my nose and twisted it until the blood began to run again. "I gotta good idea," he said. "I'm gonna tie a gag in your mouth and fry you inch by inch like roast pork. You're gonna be a walking water blister. You're gonna be sorry you ever heard the name Starkie."

He snapped the lighter again and held it toward my chin. Behind him the door opened and Geraldine Astley stood framed in the entrance of the bedroom, dressed in a sequined gown and looking fresh as a down goddess. I took a second look. She was also stewed to the gills and raring to go. I realised for the first time that she was a genuine mental deficient. There was an atrophied expression to her I hadn't noticed in her brother's bedroom.

She said: "Why doesn't someone come in and be nice to me?" Her giggle was like a bed of thistles. She came forward

147

into the room and saw me and her expression didn't change. She turned to Starkie. "Did my mother send him to collect me? Why doesn't she leave me alone?"

"Beat it," Starkie snarled. "Get outta here."

I said: "Did you read any good books lately, honey?"

Her face got perceptibly brighter. "Oh, it's you. Oh, I didn't recognise you."

"That's because they're trying to shorten my long nose," I said. "They're jealous."

The giggle came back. "Lofty has a long nose," she tittered.

Starkie spat out an oath and wheeled round and gave her hefty push. His face was twisting in horror at her. "Beat it, you lousy whore," he gritted. "Before I kick you out."

She staggered back against the wall and stayed a while, straightening herself. She came right back at him, slinking, smiling, voluptuous as a box of caterpillars. "Be nice to me," she pleaded.

"Give me the chance, honey," I said quickly.

She took no notice. She was breathing heavily. Her body writhed and she put her arms around Starkie's waist and pulled him roughly against her. She thrust her face forward, lips parted.

It was more than he could bear. He looked as if he were about to burst into tears. When he spoke his voice sounded like a six-year-old boy's. "You rotten cow," he whimpered, and then he hit her in the face with his open hand and sent her sprawling full length back into the corner. She lay looking up at him, her eyes turned to balls of sheer hatred. She looked more insane now than mentally deficient. I played a very, very remote card.

"You stinking crumb, leave the kid alone," I snarled. "Give me the chance and watch me."

He turned his back on her and in one swinging motion brought five knuckles hard at the center of my nose. My consciousness gave a lurch. It would have been nice to slip right out again, but now I didn't want to. Instead I laughed at him, not even trying to move my head to duck the second and third blows. Oh, sure, I was the swashbuckling virile all-made type all right.

Behind him Geraldine Astley was getting slowly to her feet, taking, it seemed to me, something like seventeen years. The blows were coming rat tat tat and everything was beginning to swim. I saw her open her eyes wide, stupidly, and stare around the room. She was looking for a drink. She saw the bottle of Scotch and picked it up, and I didn't know whether I'd won or not. She took two steps forward and swung from way back and the shards of glass flew all over the room as Starkie went Gah! and plunged to the floor like a pole-axed steer. She stood looking down at him, the jagged neck of the bottle still clutched in her hand. She began to giggle.

"Sweetheart, you're wonderful," I said. "Let me get my arms round you."

Her eyes cleared a little. She brought me into focus. She murmured some incomprehensible thing about my being all bloody. She swooped down and kissed me, pressing her face hard against mine, thrusting her tongue between my mashed and gory lips. She held it for about a minute while I tried to react interested, listening to her breathing and keeping an open eye on the bottleneck in case she decided to go berserk. With that type you never know.

I said: "Get these ropes off. Let's discover what it can really be like."

She drew back, and her pretty little face was all smeared up. "I remember you," she said. "It was lovely. Did my mother send you here to get me? She's always interfering since she found out. She doesn't like me going with Lofty. She says Gerald should never have introduced us."

Starkie was snoring. There was a long oozing split reaching from one side of his scalp to the other. He wouldn't be moving for a few hours, but others might be. I said: "I'm not interested in your mother, honey. I'm interested in you. Get rid of these ropes."

She brought over the neck of the bottle. She wasn't so crazy. She went right at my wrists, sawing away with a sharp edge, giggling to herself, in anticipation. Within a minute my hands were free. She grabbed one of them and tried to get funny with it. I got the bottleneck from her and pushed her gently to one side, at the same time murmuring nice things because I didn't want her to get wild. I sawed quickly and cut my hands a couple of times. In another minute I was standing up, wondering if I'd ever get back the proper use of my arms and legs. I felt, to put it mildly, like hell. My knuckles were raw and a blister was raising on my chin.

Down on the floor Starkie gave out with an especially guttural snore. He was lying on his back with one arm under him and his legs spread wide. The last of the clan. Brother one, brother two, I said to myself, and I couldn't resist it. I balanced on my left foot, drew back my right, and kicked him with all possible force. Brother three, and well fixed. The girl beside me gave a high excited laugh. I thought I was going to vomit.

"Come on." I grabbed her arm and dragged her toward the bedroom door. She came slowly, pretending to be unwilling, building up to it. She was in for a disappointment. Inside the bedroom she reached for a switch and a small overhead light came on. The place was not designed for sleeping purposes. The walls were covered with erotic pictures. The dwarf's street clothes formed a little heap on the floor. The puking feeling came back.

"How do we get out of here?" I asked.

Her eyes flicked to a large pair of curtains that looked like they were concealing a window. She undulated into position until she was looking up into my eyes. She twined her arms around my neck and started some clever work with her hips. "No one is coming back for a long time," she said. "Be nice. Be nice."

It was impossible. For the first time in my grown life the thought of it made me sick. "Okay, let's go," I said, extricating myself. "They're gonna be good and mad at you when they find out."

She backed away, standing between me and the curtains, breathing heavy so the sequins on her gown glittered and flashed in the dim light. "I want you to be nice to me," she said between her teeth.

"Not for me," I said, "not when I'm next in line behind a dwarf. Out of the way."

She didn't move. "You'd better," she said. "You'll be sorry. I'll get even with you."

"Some other day." I reached out to brush her aside and she moved like a snake and sank her teeth into my hand. I grabbed her hair and jerked up her head. Her eyes were wide and staring and mad. Her nice lips were writhing so I could see all her teeth. I released her hair and she flung back her head and she howled like a scorched banshee. I doubted even the calypso downstairs would be able to drown that.

I didn't try to stop her. I pushed her to one side and snatched at the curtains. I fumbled at the concealed door and hurtled down the stairs beyond. She came after, still yelling. I jumped the stairs three at a time, scared to death the exit at the bottom would be locked.

There was a door halfway down. A burst of laughter and applause came from behind it, They hadn't heard her yet, but they soon would. She was coming faster now, shrieking epithets that would have shamed a bargee. I didn't wait. I hurtled on. I slammed my shoulder against the door at the bottom and shot straight through, almost stretching my length on the snowy sidewalk. The cold dug into my raw flesh like acid.

It was a side street with a dead end. Fifteen yards away

from me the crowd on St. Catherine Street was moving slowly by. A cop angled past, swinging his stick, which was fine. I only had to shout for assistance and within a month he'd be a sergeant and I'd be serving a bum rap behind the wall of St. Vincent de Paul. Frankisson or a cooked up story from the Romilly would see to that. They couldn't miss. I got up and ducked back inside the door, pulling it behind me. Geraldine Astley was opening her mouth for another yell.

I clocked her—not hard, but enough to make her sink to the ground with a soft sigh. I opened the door and peered out. The crowd was milling by. The cop had gone. I offered up a prayer and it was answered. A cab coming east backed into the side street to turn around and go back west. I called and it stopped. I couldn't whistle. I hotfooted it over and scrambled into the back. The cabbie didn't even look round.

"Drive," I said, "fast. Montcalm. What time is it?"

"Nearly eleven." He let in the clutch.

The cop was standing just around the corner, still swinging his stick. He had one of those faces that never get to be beyond a constable, but all the same he looked decent enough, like he had a wife and a couple of kids and a comfortable mind. It wasn't his fault that at the moment I hated the guts of him and all like him. He couldn't help it that I was unable to call on him for help.

I sat well back and dabbed at my face, trying to clear it up before I saw Tessie. I didn't have anywhere else to go. I had to sit around somewhere and try to think. I was brassed off.

Marian Remington would have been to the Windsor Station and departed long since.

## 20

I sat at the breakfast table, logy and blue as hell. I said to Tessie, "Okay, so what happened after I got here last night?"

She said: "Don't be mad at me. I slipped a Mickey in your drink soon after you came in. I put you to bed. You were starting to babble. You were a mess. I sat up half the night putting icebags and iodine on your face. You still look like hell, only now it seems to be coming mainly from inside you. What's on your mind?"

"I feel fine."

"Liar. Tell your old Aunt Tessie what's up."

"Trouble," I said. "Things. The cops. This whole damned city."

"You can't mean Montreal—not the Paris of North America?" she grinned.

"It makes me puke," I said savagely. "Look at it. An illuminated cross stuck up on the mountain, street after street full of the reverend clergy, a self-congratulatory city council, pious editorials in all the newspapers, and as much vice and aberration and corruption as any city this side of Port Said. One level stinking and the other level smirking, and in between a layer of supposed public servants trying to stuff their greasy pockets with graft. Oh sure, we have a vice probe every decade or so. It goes on and on, year after year, and then finally it peters out under the sheer dead weight of its own evasive evidence. A few honest officials are disgraced, a few more get eased gently out of their jobs, a couple of writs for slander are issued and settled out of court, and everyone sighs with relief and goes right back to smirking abnormal. Gah! It makes my gorge jump. And to think that not so long ago this used to be a country of clear eyed pioneers."

"Away!" Tessie said, laughing. "They all drank like hell and their eyes were bloodshot from the age of fourteen. And don't kid me. You love Montreal."

"Sure I do. So what?"

"You're just mad this morning."

"No," I told her, and I meant it. "This is what I do when I get scared. I'm up to my eyes in something and I don't

153

know what it is. I start out by taking a job as nursemaid to a nineteen-year-old pansy and wind up with three murders, a couple of beatings up and every cop in the city out for my scalp. I don't like it. I know less where I'm going now than when I started."

She looked at me, a little scared herself. "You been annoying the boys again?"

"Mainly Frankisson," I said. "I had to. I can't talk. I'm protecting a client."

"Hooey!" she exploded. "You did that once before and then discovered the client wouldn't have cared a fish's tit. How do you know this one'll care. If you know anything, go and tell your pal Masson."

"Impossible," I said. "A rule of the profession."

She banged her hands together and she was good and mad. "You men make me sick with your silly damned games. Give you a uniform or set of rules or anything else that should be important only to a school kid and you immediately get a stupid look on your faces and start acting like small boys who've just read their first adventure story—prattling on about honor and duty and the rest of that rubbish. Three murders on your hands and one of them your best friend and you sit there whining about the rules of the profession. Nuts! Thank God we women have more intelligence."

I said: "My client's a woman."

"Then get in touch with her and tell her what you're going to do. She'll understand."

"I doubt it," I said.

"Try."

I went to the phone and called Miss Lindsay and asked of there'd been any calls for me. There hadn't. I hung up, and shrugged.

"Well, why don't you get in touch with your client?"

"No can do. Her mother would have me arrested. I'd be in a worse mess."

Tessie heaved me aside with one of her hips. "What's the name and number? I'll get her."

"Don't be so damned protective," I snapped. "I'm not your little boy."

"If you only knew," she said, grinning. "The name and number. Give."

She dialled. She sat there looking very good and very beautiful, waiting for the phone to ring at the other end. She did it well. She said, "Miss Marian Remington, please," just as if she were an equal, which by God she wasn't—being twenty or thirty times better than any female I could meet up on the hill. She paused and listened. She turned her head to me, a rueful look on her face. "Oh," she said, "So Marian is her bath. Another half hour? I see. Thank you."

"Get Mrs. Remington," I whispered.

"Then might I speak to Mrs. Remington, please?"

She handed me the phone. Faintly I heard the clacking footsteps come echoing across the hall. The warm, musical voice said, "Hello?"

I talked fast. I said: "I know now about Geraldine and what you meant by asking if I was trying to blackmail you. I wasn't. But I suggest you send the kid away somewhere for a cure. She was down there again last night. Did she get home?"

All the warmth evaporated. "Oh, it's you again, Mr. Garfin. The maid told me it was a woman."

"One of my numerous disguises," I said. "I use them all the time. I guess your daughter got home or you'd sound more worried. How about your son?"

She said: "I dislike intensely being rude to anyone, but my husband has told me that under no circumstances should I talk to you again. Good morning, Mr. Garfin."

"Spread the word," I said. "I'm just off to talk to the cops."

The phone went dead.

Tessie ran her fingers through my hair. "That's my Mike. Now toddle off to the police station."

"You mean fly off, don't you, like a little pigeon? It'll be lovely. The cops are not interested in getting anyone but me. They'll be very pleased to help me hang myself."

"Then go to the Mounties. Tom was one of their boys."

"The Mounties wouldn't touch me with a twenty foot grappling hook. Someday I'll tell you all about it."

"Don't be so damned leery, you stupid French mick," she shouted. "Are you gonna sit around and not talk until somebody shuts your mouth for good?" She was suddenly so mad that the tears stood in her eyes. "I don't look so good in black, damn you! It makes me look as fat as a pig."

"I'll buy you black underwear and check," I said. "Here. See if you can get in touch with Masson. He's probably at the station. The guy never sleeps."

She took the phone. It must have been a young sounding voice at the other end because unconsciously she began to flutter her eyelids. She waited a while and said, "Yes, I see," and hung up. She said: "They tell me he's down at the morgue."

"All the better. It'll make what I say seem less official." I got up and kissed the end of her nose, and I heard the street door rattle. Marguerite came in, lit. She wasn't looking so good.

"Some party!" she exclaimed, dropping wearily into a chair. "It didn't start till two and it's still going on." She grinned up at me. "I've got some bad news for you. You've lost your second string. Little Felicity Magworth went home around four with a young guy in the garment trade. It looked like permanent."

"Where does he live?"

She spread her hands. "No idea. I'll keep you posted. I'll be seeing her around. Was it important?"

"It doesn't matter," I said.

The smile left her face. She slumped deeper into the chair. "You're right, it doesn't. Nothing matters. There's plenty more people in the world, and they come and go, don't they? They come quick and they go quick, don't they?" A great sob wrenched up from inside her and she began to weep. I went out, closing the door quietly behind me, and Tessie was murmuring exactly the right things in a soothing tone. Tessie's okay.

## 21

I first got my car back from the Mounties, signing my name to about six sheafs of paper while the guys drifted in and out just for the pleasure of giving me a hostile look. I didn't blame them. I was on their side. I didn't like me very much this morning either. Especially not when I got behind the wheel and thought about Tom driving the heap on that last night. But someone had fixed the broken skid chain. It made me feel a little better. Not much.

The weather was continuing bitter cold. At that, the inside of the morgue seemed colder. A couple of cops were standing around in the ante-room, and they told me Masson was out back with the slabs. They said I could go through, and then I got the looks again, only they couldn't do it as well as the Mounties. Also it affected me differently. I thought they stank.

Masson was standing with his foot up on a hard chair, talking to a sergeant and a constable who had notebooks. My cherished pal Dr. Armand, was down at the back, pulling a sheet off one of the stiffs. Masson looked up and nodded at me, and his eyebrows flicked as he got a look at my mashed face. "In a while, Mike," he said, and turned back to the sergeant. "Continue."

The sergeant looked back at his book. "Their names are William Macy and Robert Forrest. They work for the Fortin Ice Company. This morning at eight o'clock they were cutting blocks of ice from the river to be delivered later to a customer at—"

"Okay for that," Masson interrupted impatiently. "What happened?"

"Nothing much. The body came up from under the ice and they dragged it out and called us. They got no idea who the guy is. They got no idea about nothing."

"Not like you," Masson said tartly.

"Well, we're working on it, Chief, but it's tough. There wasn't a stitch on him, and with his head bashed like that— Anyway, we're working on it. Going over the surrounding ground with a fine comb."

Masson raised his voice. "How long's he been dead, Doctor?"

"Hard to tell. Remember, this guy's been refrigerated." Armand looked up from the slab, saw me, started to sneer, and decided to let it ride. "But there's a couple of things I can tell you. One, he was between twenty-five and thirty, and two, he didn't get these head injuries under the ice. Rule out all possibilities of suicide. This baby was neatly and very methodically scalped. Whoever did it also caved in his skull and worked on his face with a knife."

"Indians," the constable volunteered hopefully.

Masson gave him a look of withering contempt. "Get a chart of the teeth," he said, "and we'll canvas all the dentists. There's only about half a million in the district. Hell and damnation, the guy probably came from Oshawa or Medicine Hat and was just here for the day. Let's take a look at him."

"You'll find nothing more," Armand said huffily. "There are no scars or other identifying marks."

"Nevertheless, we'll take a look." Masson went over

to the slab, followed by the constable who was still trying to recover from the remark about Indians. I trailed along behind, hoping to see Armand beaten down, willing to help it along if possible. He was watching my approach with a cold eye. The sneer came up. I said:

"How's the baby racket?"

"Cut it out!" Masson snapped. "Shut up, Mike, or you wait outside."

Armand held his tongue. Masson peered at the body. "Skull crushed in," he remarked.

"I told you. And it wasn't done by ice."

"I wonder why they wanted to scalp him."

Armand was looking into the mouth. "You'll need to think again, Chief. They've knocked out most of his teeth. Smart boys."

Sure, I thought, and cold-blooded. The face, what was left of it, was an almost shapeless mass of chilled meat. The nose had been cut off and one eye was forced from its socket by a heavy blow. The whole head was raw where the hair had been removed.

I ran my eyes over the torso. He'd been a biggish guy— big hands, big feet. The muscles of the chest and shoulders, particularly of the stomach, were strong and well defined. Around the groin the pubic hair had coppery tint in its darkness.

That would explain why they scalped him. Too easily recognisable.

I went back to the hands. Before anyone could object I picked up the right one. The skin was drawn from being in the water—evenly drawn except for one small area between the first and second joint of one finger. Armand started to protest. I said:

"Could this guy have had red hair?"

Armand turned his head away, not answering.

Masson was looking at me with narrowed eyes. He

tapped Armand on the shoulder. "Could the corpse have been red-headed, Doctor?"

Armand blew up. "I sometimes wonder who's running this lousy police force," he snarled.

"Well, now you know," Masson said calmly. "I am. Just answer the question."

I got a shaft of venom and Armand bent down for a closer scrutiny. After about a minute he growled, grudging, "He could have I suppose."

"You were a few years out on the age," I told him. "The kid was only nineteen."

That did it. He lost his temper completely and started to yell, "I don't allow any goddam layman to tell me my job—"

"The mark on his right hand," I interrupted, "is the remains of a blister caused by a cigarette lighter." I turned to Masson. "I may be wrong. I usually am. Where's the phone?"

He took me into a small office and stood watching me dial, looking placid but betraying himself by the way he shifted his weight from one foot to the other. The voice from the other end came smooth and impersonal, the ideal and very expensive receptionist.

"Mr. Remington, please," I said.

"I'm terribly sorry, sir, but Mr. Remington is away in New York."

"Then you'd better get him back fast," I said. "This is the police. We can be over in three minutes."

"Oh." Her voice sounded as if her training had not included a situation like this. She recovered immediately. "Excuse me, sir, but I have to check all Mr. Remington's calls to prevent him being unduly bothered. I'll put you through at once."

She took her time. There was a faint click, followed by a long pause, and then he came onto the line, smooth and urbane and only faintly inquisitive. "Can I help you? I understand this is the police."

160

"In a way," I said. "It's Garfin."

There was another pause and I heard him laughing. "Clever of you, Garfin. Everyone but my intimates thinks me in New York. How did you guess I was in town?"

"Guess is right," I said. "When your wife told me you'd advised her not to speak to me under any circumstances it sounded like immediate contact and not a long-distance phone."

"Did she speak as strongly as that?" He sounded genuinely surprised. "I'm afraid Mrs. Remington is overwrought about something. You seem somehow to be mixed up in it. I merely told her not to have anything to do with you if it upsets her." He cleared his throat, hesitating. "I don't wish to be obtrusive, Garfin, but is there anything I should know? Could we have lunch together and talk about it?"

"Sooner than that," I said. "I'm at the morgue. You'd better get here right away."

"The morgue?"

"The morgue. Captain Masson of the City Police is with me. Do you want him to invite you?"

"I don't understand," Remington said. "You make it sound important. I'll come immediately."

I hung up and turned to Masson. He offered me a cigarette, staring at me long and hard over the burning match. "I hope to God you're right," he said, "otherwise this'll put you so deep in the merde you'll never get out. There are other phones in this building. Right now I figure your pal Dr. Armand is getting in touch with your chum Mr. Frankisson. It'll be a nice party."

"Can he pinch me for anything if I'm wrong?"

"Obstructing justice," Masson suggested experimentally. "No, not that. Creating a public nuisance. No, too trivial. Frankisson's going to find a way to drop the whole book on you."

"Nice man," I said. "I'm ever so much looking forward to seeing him again."

161

And I hadn't long to wait. I stubbed out my half-finished cigarette and went back among the slabs and Frankisson was already there, holding a whispered conversation with Armand that cut off abruptly as I walked in. He approached me with eyes like gelatinized vitriol. His voice hadn't a single inflection, one way or the other.

"You've identified this corpse?"

"Not definitely. I think it's a kid named Gerald Astley. I've just asked Colin Remington, his stepfather, to come down for a positive identification."

"Colin Remington? Canada Stock? Remington Imports?"

"That's him."

Frankisson bared his teeth in a mirthless smile. "Murder in Montreal," he said softly, "is a low class business. The rich are seldom murdered, and the very rich, never. Could this be another little example of your chicanery?"

"Big word," I said. "We'll wait."

"And you claim Gerald Astley was around nineteen?"

Armand came running like a poodle at a post. "The victim was between twenty-five and thirty. In view of the bone pliability and the general physical development I can state that unequivocally. Between twenty-five and thirty."

"He was leading an adult life," I said. "A big boy for his age. You may be wrong. So may I. Shut up. Your whining voice makes me sick."

"Do I have to put up with this?" Armand demanded, white to the lips.

Frankisson's eyes were like the twin granite doors to my own tomb. He said nothing. We all looked at each other in silence, with Masson moving from one foot to the other, and suddenly the door behind us opened and a shuffling attendant ushered in Remington.

He was wearing a gray business suit, a plain tie, a four-hundred-dollar topcoat, and a pearl colored homburg that would have looked ridiculous on anyone else this weather but only made him look better than usual. He nodded to me pleasantly, peeled off his fur lined suede gloves, and looked around with a polite smile of inquiry until he eyes lighted on Masson's uniform. "Ah, Captain," he said. "You wanted to see me?"

Frankisson stepped forward, holding out a hand. "I'm in charge here, sir. Name of Frankisson."

"Ah yes, I've heard of you, of course." Remington made it a compliment, shaking the extended hand warmly. "In what way can I possibly help?"

"I'm not sure that you can, sir," Frankisson said. "This is not a police idea. Garfin phoned you without my knowledge. He thinks you might be able to identify a corpse."

"Do what?" Remington flashed me an incredulous look and turned back to Frankisson, eyebrows forming a curve of disbelief. "I—of course I'd like to help. But why does Mr. Garfin think I can?"

"See the body first, sir." Frankisson took him by the arm. "Prepare yourself for a shock. It's not a particularly pleasant sight."

Remington had removed his hat and was holding it by the brim, like a well bred mourner at a society funeral. Armand was standing at the head of the slab, clutching the edge of the sheet as if her were a conjuror about to reveal a bowl of goldfish. He said, "Are you ready, sir? and when Remington nodded he whipped off the cloth with a flourish.

There was a sharp gasp of horror and Remington automatically took a step back in revulsion. He swayed and turned pale and I thought he was going to faint. Then he recovered himself and straightened, moving his arm unconsciously to shake off Frankisson's hand. There was a long silence while he looked at the body. His lips were drawn in to prevent them quivering. Finally he spoke, and his voice was damped to a whisper. He said:

"Who is this supposed to be?"

The elated triumph on Armand's face almost blinded me. Frankisson turned a cold stare. "Speak up, Garfin."

I said, "It's your stepson, Gerald Astley." My voice was faltering. I sounded phony as a three-dollar bill, even to myself. I saw bewilderment and instant rejection follow each other across Remington's face. He steeled himself and looked back to the slab.

We waited. Armand said: "I understand your son was nineteen, sir. I judge the corpse to be nearer thirty.

Remington ignored him, went on staring, beginning to shake his head slowly. I moved closer to him and suddenly he wheeled on me.

"I don't know what your game is, Garfin," he said quietly, "or even if you're playing one, but this body is certainly not my stepson, nor anything like him. He was slimmer, smaller. He was still a boy, and this appears to be the body of a grown man. I believe you saw Gerald only once, which may account for the mistake. It is nevertheless a regrettable one."

They were moving in on me. I said quickly, "Okay, where's Gerald now? Produce him."

A faint flush spread over Remington's face. He looked at Frankisson. "Has Garfin any right to question me?"

"None whatever," Frankisson said grimly. "I'm sorry you've been put to this bother."

"Thank you. I'll gladly tell you anything you to know about my stepson. He is a troublesome boy. At present he is in Toronto, on a drinking bout I fear. I am considering sending him abroad."

"There is no need to tell us this, sir," Frankisson said. "I shall be looking for explanations from another quarter. May I see you to your car?"

Remington put on his pearly hat. He spoke of me as if I wasn't there. "There's one small thing, Mr. Frankisson. Garfin has been upsetting my wife of late by constantly phoning the house and attempting to see her. I wish her to know nothing of this morning's incident until I can tell her myself. If you could advise Mr. Garfin not to attempt to communicate with her—"

"Certainly," Frankisson said briskly. "If you'd like to press charges I think we can commit him as a public nuisance."

"Oh no, nothing like that. I think he means well."

"I'll see," Frankisson said. Armand laughed. I chalked it up against him. Frankisson and Remington headed for the door, their demeanour changed now that everything was settled. Frankisson said, "I was reading the other day, Mr. Remington, of your latest donation to the Victoria Hospital." They went outside.

Masson got between me and the smirking Armand, just in case. "What did you want to see me about in the first place?" he asked.

"Nothing," I said. "A mistake. So far you've no reason— or at least no warrant—for holding me here. See you later."

I went out fast, into the the office where I'd made the phone call and through the window into the alley. I cat-footed down the side of the morgue toward the street and peeped round the corner in time to see Remington and Frankisson have the final handshake. From their exchanged smiles I guessed they'd got onto the Rotary Club or the Kiwanis. I ducked back, counted a slow fifteen, and looked again. They were both gone. I ran to my car, got in on the far side, and started at thirty-five. I was in a hurry to get away. Times like this and the mere sight of my face could persuade Frankisson to issue a warrant. I didn't want that. I had ideas crowding my head and needed a spell to work them out. I hoped Frankisson would take his own sweet tormenting time pulling me in.

But Masson was right to say I was in the merde. I was deep in it. I could smell it.

## 22

"She'll not come," Miss Lindsay burred, reaching out and lifting Sir Walter Scott onto her lap. "She sounded too cautious."

I lit another cigarette, my seventh, stubbing out the sixth in the ashtray. "Tell me again what she said."

"But you were sitting there. I told her I could give her some news of her son Gerald if she'd come over right away, and said not to tell anyone. That's when she got cautious."

"Not with your voice," I said. "You sound like lavender and lace and ginger cookies in a jar. Did she seem familiar with the address?"

"I'm sure she wasn't." Miss Lindsay gripped Sir Walter's tail and ran her hand from base to tip. The cat gave an ecstatic stretch. Miss Lindsay patted its head absent-mindedly. "Mike," she said, "are you in trouble again?"

I would have answered on a sour note. I didn't get time. The front door bell rang briefly and Sir Walter leapt to the floor and trotted up the passage, tail up, as he always does. Miss Lindsay started to flutter. "What do I say to her? Shall I show her to your sitting room? Do you want me to keep out of the way?"

"Calm down," I said. "Bring her in here. And stick around."

I heard the door open and a polite murmur of something about how cold it was. An expensive scent crept through the house, strengthening as Mrs. Remington came down the passage. I got out of the armchair. She was saying, "I don't quite understand, Miss uh Miss Lindsay," and then she was confronting me, eyes gone wide, lips parted.

She looked beautiful and ill and so deathly white that the faint make-up sat on her face like a mask. She lifted a gloved hand to her cheek and said quietly, "Oh, I see." She turned round to where Miss Lindsay was blocking the passage and added, "Please excuse me. I must leave now."

I said: "Sit down, Mrs. Remington. This is important."

She remained standing, addressing the Lindsay. "I'm sure you didn't know what he was making you do. I'm sorry. I wish nothing whatever to do with him. He is deceitful and dangerous."

And then there should have been a wild skirl of bag-pipes, for the Lindsay reverted completely to type and became one of her tough, black browed ancestors. She stuck her hands on her hips and her five-feet-two looked suddenly like a scowling six-feet-eight. She said: "Well, of all the cheek, talking about him like that. Listen, missus, you'd better change your tune right this instant if you expect to become a friend of mine. Him telling me you're a nice woman and everything, and the first thing you do is start calling him names that your own common sense should tell you are wrong. Look at him, woman! Look at his poor sweet face that's got so knocked about. Can you believe the silly things you're saying?"

She was very funny. She was also somehow impressive. I didn't laugh, and neither did Mrs. Remington. Her gaze came slowly to rest on my face and I tried to compose it into an expression of sweetness. I felt I wasn't doing so well. But something must have tripped the switch. She went paler than ever. "What is it, Mr. Garfin?" she asked quietly.

This was going to be tough. She had me marked down as a dangerous pest and what I needed to say sounded insane. I tried to think of a sensible, less shocking way. There didn't seem to be one. I said: "Will you trust me, Mrs. Remington? I want you to do something that'll be pretty damned unpleasant. I wouldn't ask if there was anyone else, but there's no one. Will you come?"

She blinked her eyes twice, slowly. She spoke, and her lips were barely moving. "This lady told me on the phone that it's something to do with Gerald."

"It is," I said.

Sir Walter Scott rubbed against her legs. She looked down at him, then stooped suddenly and stroked his back. The cat began to purr. She straightened up, looking me directly in the eyes. "I do trust you, Mr. Garfin," she said. "I think I always have. Please don't ask me any questions. Let me do whatever you wish and then take me home."

I nodded briefly. "Whatever you say. Let's go. Did you bring a car?"

"Miss Lindsay said to keep it secret. I came by cab."

"Fine," I said, and took her arm, perhaps more tightly than was necessary. We went along the passage with the Lindsay and Sir Walter fetching up in the rear. At the door Mrs. Remington held out her hand.

"You have a lovely cat," she said. "I like cats. Thank you for phoning me."

"Very welcome, I'm sure," the Lindsay answered, looking like the queen of the Kelpies. "Come again, dear, when you've more time. We'll have a talk over a cup of tea. Do you read ghost stories?"

"Sometimes. You're very sweet. Goodby."

We drove downtown in complete silence. I snuffed up her perfume and wondered how the hell I was going to break the news to her. I stole a look at her profile, drawn and composed and beautiful, framed against a background of moving buildings. I liked what I saw. My hands were very tight on the wheel.

One block from the morgue I pulled into a side street and cut the motor. She looked at me with something in her eyes that was like resignation. I said, "This is going to be rotten so take a hold on yourself. The city morgue is just up the street there. I want you to go in and ask to see the body that was brought in this morning—the one that was under the ice. I don't think there'll be any difficulty, but if so say that Captain Masson sent you. When you've taken a good look come back here and tell me who it is, if you know."

I expected protest, contempt, flat refusal—any reaction but the one I got. There was not the faintest trace of surprise. She continued looking at me without moving a muscle for fully thirty seconds, just staring into my eyes. At last she spoke, and her voice was utterly weary. "Aren't you coming with me, Mr. Garfin?" she asked.

"I'm sorry, it's not practical." I reached over and opened the door for her. "I really am sorry, Mrs. Remington."

"Yes," she said, "I can see you are. I'll be as quick as I can, Mr. Garfin. Please wait for me."

She got out of the car and disappeared round the corner. I shut the door and began to doubt her. I leaned back and lit a cigarette and wondered if she would send Frankisson back in her place. For that matter, any cop would do. There wasn't one of them who wouldn't delight in sticking me on the hooks, especially if Mrs. Remington pitched them a yarn. It may have been plain common sense that made her act agreeably back at the house. If I was dangerous as at first she claimed, then it must have seemed to her that she was in a tight spot.

There was another risk. Frankisson might still be at the morgue. Or Masson. Or both. Swell if she should tell them Captain Masson sent her when he was standing right at her shoulder and she hadn't recognised him. He wouldn't take it up, but the others would, and quick. I was counting on the fact that policemen, no less than anyone else, don't hang around morgues any longer than they can help.

I finished my cigarette and lit another. I was scared. The pieces were beginning to fall into place, and the solution was enough to dry anybody's juices. One thing was certain—I wasn't going to be believed unless there was some corroborative talking done, and at the moment that looked like a remote possibility. Unless Mrs. Remington turned out to be exactly what I had thought of her in the first place. Unless she was at the moment getting such a shock that her tongue would be loosened.

I tried to console myself by tooting up how much I had made out of the deal so far. A hundred from Mrs. Remington, three from him, and two-eighty from my present employer, Marian Remington. Six-eighty altogether. On the debit side was two-twenty paid to Snowy Etheridge, bruised kidneys, a mashed face, and the fact that every authority in town would have a fiesta on the day I hanged. I could make as much, and with less trouble, working the mines up in Ungava. I wondered, and not for the first time, if I was in the right profession.

She was away for maybe fifteen minutes. I'd got around to thinking she'd not intended to visit the morgue at all but just hailed a cab and gone straight home, when I saw her come around the corner. She was walking very straight and steady. Her face was the color of the snow on which she trod. She came unhesitantly to the car and got in beside me. "Drive me home," she said, and sat very upright, head averted.

We drove without saying anything. The shock had been too great, or there was no shock at all. I went by a roundabout route, driving slowly to give her time to make a decision, if one needed to be made. I turned into Sherbrooke Street and bowled along at about twenty. The clock over the Roddick Gate said ten after twelve. A mob of kids were coming off the McGill campus from their lectures. I pulled up to let some of them over the road to the Student Union and the whole herd surged across.

They were the usual kids, dressed in everything from fur coats to sweaters and scarves. They made a lot of noise and showed a lot of teeth, and most of them looked as if they were having a good time. I honked my horn and nosed forward. A girl with auburn hair ducked around the fender and smiled back over her shoulder. She was cute. I crept through the crowd and opened up a little.

Mrs. Remington gave a convulsive sob and fell sideways, burying her head in my lap. She was weeping like her heart was broken, and maybe that was so. I drew over to the side of the road and stopped the car. Few people were passing. I lifted her up and took her face on my shoulder and put my arms around her shaking frame. I got a quick picture of what it would be like to be married to Mrs. Remington, and it would have been nice. I said to her, "Take it easy, honey. I'm sorry. It was Gerald, wasn't it?"

Her head nodded with agonised slowness against my coat. Her weeping made no sound. I took a handkerchief from my pocket and thrust it into her hand, putting the tips of my fingers under her chin and lifting her head. Oh yes, she was beautiful, even weeping. Behind the tears her eyes were the color of sapphires.

She said: "Please, please forgive me. I can't help it."

"Don't mind," I said. "Don't mind at all. If there'd only been a way to spare you the shock."

Her face was numb. She shook her head, and her dignity was wonderful. "No," she whispered. "No, it wasn't really. When my husband told me about it I had a feeling it was really Gerald." The tears welled over. She buried her face in my handkerchief.

"So he mentioned it to you," I said. "You were expecting it. You're a brave woman, Mrs. Remington." I waited until the bout was passed and she lifted her head again. "Did you tell the police?"

She shook her head, quickly, as if trying to cast something from her brain. "I couldn't. I have to think first. There must be some explanation, there must be."

"He was your son," I said.

"No, but I can't. It's all so confused. My husband will be agonised when he discovers his mistake. He loved Gerald, I know he did."

"You have to tell someone," I said to her. "Will you tell me?"

She paused a long time. She opened her mouth and shut it again. She took out a small gold compact from her handbag and dabbed nervously at her face, covering the tearstains with a thin coating of powder. She looked as if hse was recovered, everywhere but in her agonised eyes. When she had finished she returned my handkerchief. She said, "Take me home now, Mr. Garfin."

I went along Sherbrooke and up the mountain and she remained mute. I drove to the top of the hill on which she lived, turned around and came down again, drawing to a stop a little past her house. She reached for the door-handle. "I don't know, Mr. Garfin," she said. "I must think it out."

"I'll be home all day," I told her. "The phone is under Miss Lindsay's name. I'll be waiting for you to call. I'll be with you within ten minutes."

"Yes," she replied, and I saw the tears spring back into her eyes.

I said: "Mrs. Remington, what's your first name?"

"Vivian."

"That's nice. Vivian. I like it. Listen, Vivian: make sure I'm the first one you talk to about this. Or about anything. Don't tell anyone that you know about Gerald. Not anyone."

The tears were coming down her face, but I knew by the hardening of her voice that she understood what I was getting at. "When I have convinced myself," she said, "as you seem to have done, I shall call you immediately."

"Good," I said. "Does your husband come home for lunch?"

"No."

"Well, goodby then. Call me soon."

She got out of the car and slammed the door and walked off without another word. I didn't look back. I took off the hand brake and coasted down the hill and drove home, thinking that her children were not a bit like her, and what a crumb her first husband must have been to beget a couple like that on her. Certainly they must take after him. She was too nice.

Miss Lindsay was waiting for me, burning with curiosity. "Didn't the lady come back with you?" She was disappointed.

I shook my head. "I'm hoping to see her again this afternoon."

"Such a nice woman," the Lindsay said. "Beautiful. She has something about her. Is she an actress?"

I hadn't thought of that. "I don't know," I said, "but I hope not. By God, I hope not."

# 23

I ate a large lunch, slowly, while Miss Lindsay tried to soothe me by describing her childhood in Scotland. Then I tried lounging around to figure things out. The figuring went reasonably well: all I needed was a dead loss. Each of my nerves was attached to a wire, and whenever I arrived at a new conclusion the wires twitched. I was a grasshopper with the palsy, but I didn't want to take a drink. I had an idea there was still an awful lot of day to go yet. I couldn't have been righter.

I was half expecting a call from Marian Remington. It didn't come. I was half expecting a visit from Frankisson and his boys, or from some of the yeggs at the Romilly. They didn't come either. During the past hours I'd lost sight of the idea of the Quebec Crime Syndicate, mentioned by the dear departed Maisie, but now I was even expecting some sort of manifestation from them. Which made four half-expectings and totalled two whole expectations. No wonder I was beginning to twitch.

I guess Maisie's body was under the ice, too. A popular place, and room for plenty more. The river is long and mostly deserted and stretches out into the country. All you need is a pickaxe and a saw—and the hole freezes over in something like fifteen minutes. I thought about it all very deeply and began to get the chills. The guy on the lunchtime newscast had said the cold was about to break, that the temperature was due to jump. I didn't believe him. The weather can act like crazy in Montreal, but when I looked from the window the world had never looked colder, nor more permanently so.

At thirty-five minutes after four, when I'd given up hope, the phone rang. When she spoke I knew that she and I were hovering around the same conclusions. Her voice was hard, with no trace of tears. She said: "I've made up my mind, Mr. Garfin. I want to talk to you."

"Fine," I said.

"There's a great deal of smoke and very little flame and it doesn't altogether make sense—it's too difficult to believe. But perhaps you can convince me. Perhaps you know something that will enable us to go to the police together. I am not a stupid woman, and I was told one lie too many."

"They were a little too clever, that's all."

"Clever?" Her voice was steel. "More than that. I believed everything, even that Gerald was in Toronto. What other lies are there, that I don't even dream of?"

"It's going to be hard for you."

"My son was murdered. There is nothing harder than that. I mean to have my revenge no matter who suffers. Come over immediately, Mr. Garfin. I shall be waiting upstairs in the library. I'll tell the maid to expect you." She paused. "I can't talk any longer on the phone; there are four extensions in the house."

"Be right there," I said and hung up. Miss Lindsay was at my elbow, nursing the cat.

"Give her my regards," she said. "Don't forget your overshoes."

"Sure enough." I put on my hat and coat and went into my own room to check my gun so as not to scare the Lindsay.

174

I filled a pocket with spare shells, called goodby, and went out to the car. I drove like hell for the mountain. I hadn't worn my overshoes, after all.

I was feeling good. It looked like the beginning of the end. Also I was about to see Vivian Remington again. I felt so good that I switched on the radio, and not even the frenetic announcer on CJAD could annoy me. The band played a hopped-up version of Little White Lies. I began to whistle.

The day was drawing in, a dusk that turned the snow to a carpet of pale blue. Maybe the cold was easing, but the passers-by looked frozen as ever, hands in pockets, ears in collars. I got in a few tricky whistling trills that I'd forgot I could do, and soared up the hill, revving down to approach the Remington driveway, preparing to turn in.

The big stationary Cadillac was facing out, almost blocking the entrance. I continued up the hill, turned round, and pulled up outside the house with the car nose pointing down. I got out and jaunted up the driveway. Beaver face answered the door.

She looked a little more respectful today. Not much. "Mrs. Remington's expecting you," she announced. "She's up in the second floor library."

I handed her my hat and coat and she didn't seem to like the way I did it. "Anyone else at home?" I asked.

Her eyebrows went up, indicating it was none of my damned business. "I'm sure I don't know," she said, "I only work here." She turned with a sniff and wandered off toward a cloakroom.

"Don't bother to show me up. Where is this library?"

She was liking me less and less. "Second floor," she snapped, "right at the front of the house. Try not to knock anything over on your way up."

"You and I must have a date some night," I told her. "I like a girl with spirit."

She gave a final toss of her head and disappeared behind

175

a door. There was a rattling of coathangers and a banging sound, and I wondered if she was jumping up and down on my hat, just for fun. I went on up the stairs.

The dusklight was coming in the windows and fighting the electric light, already switched on, making the modern paintings on the wall look like nightmares in an abbatoir. A silence had all at once settled on the house. The plushy carpet gave my footfalls the muffled sound they get in funeral parlors. I reached the top of the stairs, turned right, and padded along the landing. A door was ajar in front of me, revealing an unlighted room, one wall of which I could vaguely see as lined with books.

I knocked gently and the door swung a little farther open. I waited and there was no reply. Suddenly the stillness in the house had become hot and oppressive, and I took a deep gulp of air. I said softly, "Mrs. Remington," and knocked again, pushing the door wide. The roaring sound of a car engine came up from the street and I sprinted across the intervening space to the window and looked out. The Cadillac was disappearing fast down the hill.

I turned back into the room. Vivian Remington was sitting in a corner at a desk, waiting for me. She was waiting for all of eternity. She was dead.

I snapped on the reading light. She had fallen forward with her face on the desk, the brown hair spread out in a frame for her head. A knife was buried up to the hilt in her neck—a fancy paper knife. The blood was still flowing sluggishly, soaking the blotter on which she lay, spreading in a slow patch over her dress. I lifted her up and looked down into her eyes. The sapphires were stagnant water, the dignity had become the frozen hauteur of the tomb. I released her gently and let her lie, not touching the knife.

It was less than a minute since I'd entered the library. There might be still be time to catch the Cadillac—especially if the driver felt as confident as there was every reason to be.

Never had a trick been so neatly turned. Never, surely, was there such a sitting duck as myself. I straightened up and wheeled on my heel, prepared to run.

Beaver face stood petrified on the threshold, a tray of teacups in her nerveless hands, eyes showing the whites all round the pupil. She sucked in her breath. The tray hit the ground and the crockery shattered. She took three backward steps and held out her hands to ward me off. Then she opened her mouth and started to scream. I wouldn't have thought the old girl had so much noise in her.

I didn't wait. I hurtled past her and down the stairs, rocketing through the front door and out into the driveway. In the car the radio was playing a June and moon tune and a guy was singing. He sounded like a castrato. I felt like one. My teeth were chattering.

But the timing was bad. The rush hour was on, and the streets packed with traffic. I waited for three out of four traffic lights, then turned south and tried St. Catherine Street. It was worse than ever. I waited for another light and went farther south, along Dorchester, only to find myself in a crawling line behind another crawling line of streetcars. I had stopped shivering now and begun to sweat. My hands on the wheel felt like I was washing them. I was heading for the Romilly Club. It was the only place I could think of.

Somewhere between Guy Street and University I heard the sirens start to wail. The boys can't resist it. I flicked the radio dial around to the police waveband and it was as I expected. I had dark brown hair, brown eyes, and a small scar on my left cheek where a bullet had once nicked me. I was six-feet-one, a hundred-and-ninety, was wearing a blue suit, and no hat or topcoat. I was driving a red coupé and they had the number. They were to exercise care because I was believed to be armed. I was wanted for the murder of Mrs. Vivian Remington. All cars.

The guy at the mike was having himself a time, and I

could visualise the general jubilation going on around him. Cheers led by Mr. Frankisson.

I was glad afterwards that the traffic crept so slowly. I had time to see the patrol car that cut across the traffic and drew up just past the escalator entrance to Central Station, squealing brakes and a dying siren. A cop was getting out as I pulled from the line and swung into the first side-street. He didn't see me. I drove up and turned into an alley. It was dark. I opened the door and got out of the car.

God, it was cold. It went right through the fabric of my suit like a million icy needles. My skin tautened, numbed, and I began to think lovingly of my topcoat hanging in the Remington closet. I reached into the back seat, got the travelling rug, rolled it into a bundle and tucked it under my arm. Then I closed the car door quietly and ran like hell. I wanted to get away from those cops.

I kept to the side streets. I was freezing. I had to do something, and quick. I worked my way back onto Dorchester, keeping my head down, and ducked inside a drugstore, feeling the warmth wrap around me. All the stools at the lunch counter were occupied. The smell of coffee filled the air. But it was no go. Every man in the place still had his topcoat on. I went over into the phone booth, keeping my face turned away. I inserted my dime and dialled Tessie. She'd get me a topcoat.

"Hello?"

"Mike here," I said.

"And the cops here," she said, and hung up.

I got out fast, unobtrusive as I could. I dodged back on a side street and into another alley. I could hear the streetcars rattling along Dorchester, one after the other. The cold was paralysing me. In the dimness I leaned against the wall and wrapped the traveling rug around me. It was only slightly less than useless. I thrust my numb hands deep into my pants pockets.

Finally I got a plan—a sketchy one, but my last hope.

Only I'd have to wait a time to put it into action. Maybe all night. And I couldn't wait here. Reason one, I'd freeze to death. Reason two, when the cops found my car they'd seal off the whole area. And maybe somebody was watching me from a window, right this moment, wondering what I was loitering for, suspecting a felony, phoning the police. I had to move, get somewhere more isolated.

I folded the rug and tried to kill the butterflies in my belly. I walked back onto Dorchester Street, and the cop was waiting on the other side of the road, a little way up, scanning the street both ways. A mob of people were opposite him, on my side, waiting for a streetcar. For a terrifying moment I didn't know where to run.

I heard the rattle and grind of wheels and a No. 65 Trolley was coming up behind me. It drew level and I loped along the sidewalk abreast of it, panting and wheezing at the icy air inside of my lungs. The streetcar pulled up, and the mob surged, and I surged with them, flailing my arms and struggling with the rest to get aboard.

I was third man on. I slapped down my thirty cents and didn't wait for my tickets. I started to fight my way to the back and I lifted my head and I stopped. A cop was standing by the rear exit, gazing dreamily out of the window.

"Get to the rear please. Down the car please."

The conductor was snapping his ritual over and over like some crazy priest. I reached up and hung on to a strap. A middle-aged woman struggled to get her arms free and accidentally hit me. A big guy in a warm looking topcoat stuck his elbow into my back and snarled something about people who wouldn't move along and make room for other people. The cop turned his head from the window and gazed with superior amusement on the raging crowd who unlike himself had had to pay for their tickets, thirty cents for three. I bent at the knees until I was the same height as the people on either side of me, and the streetcar started with a lurch.

Nobody spoke. A few fanatics were trying to read six square inches of evening newspaper. The car swayed and I swung against the knees of the girl who sat under my strap. She looked hard to see if I was getting fresh. She looked again, less interested, noticing for the first time that I was without a topcoat. She looked away, probably marking me down as an immigrant, and the car rattled on, too full to halt at other stops. The passengers swayed in unavoidable accord.

We turned north and went across St. Catherine Street, starting the long hill that enters the residential district and leaves the neon lights behind. The car halted once, twice, three times—quiet streets where the lamps glowed bright in the bitter air. People got off. The view between myself and the cop was less obstructed. He was looking out of the window again. The car slowed down, almost stopping, and I edged toward the front exit.

The driver spoke. He said: "Hey bud, you got two more tickets coming to you." He moved his handle and the streetcar stopped completely. He didn't open the door and I was stuck.

The panic went racing through me. "Not me," I said.

"Sure," I remember because you ain't wearing a coat."

"Oh yeah, that's right," I said, and held out my hand.

He hesitated. "Maybe it wasn't you. There was a hell of a rush. I thought it was you, but maybe it wasn't."

I could feel the cop's eyes burning into the back of my flimsy jacket. "Forget it," I hissed. "Open the door."

The annoyance writhed across his face. He got truculent. "No need to get funny about it," he growled, and stamped angrily on the pedal. The doors opened with a pneumatic sigh and I jumped out, clutching the traveling rug, footing it for the sidewalk. The streetcar moved off. I turned to watch it go. The cop was peering out of the back window, screwed up eyes, trying to catch a sight of me. I made for the nearest house as if I lived there.

The guy on the radio had been right; it was getting warmer. I squinted at the thermometer on the wall of the house and the temperature had risen to three degrees above zero. It was small comfort. Men have died in ten, twelve, and even twenty above. I got back onto the street, stamping my feet hard, clawing at my ears and nose in case of frostbite. Another streetcar was coming up the hill behind me. I turned into a sidestreet, away from the tracks.

They call it a mountain in Montreal, and they're proud of it. Why not? The city was named after it—Mount Royal, Montreal. But it's really little more than a glorified hill—a great illuminated cross at the summit and the upper slopes covered with trees. I walked through ascending streets, getting nearer the top, working toward the district where the Remingtons lived. Whenever an automobile passed I wheeled sharply and made for the nearest front door. When it was gone I cut diagonally across the garden and resumed my tramp. My shoes were full of snow, my feet like dead ice. Below me the lights of the city gleamed colder than diamonds.

I reached the last, the topmost residential street, up where the houses are biggest and warmest looking. I turned my back on them and hit out for the cold stark trees. In summer I would have stumbled over prostrate couples, but few people come here between November and April, none of them at night. My stumbling now was caused by snowdrifts, concealed gullies. I was wet to the knees, slowly petrifying, and through the linings of my pants pockets my hands had communicated their frozen state to my thighs. I reached the beginning line of trees and started breaking through the bracken, penetrating for about a hundred yards before I stopped. A stillness descended upon me, for which the muffled noise of the city below was only a background. A few stars had come out, high and tiny, remote and cheerless. I struck my lighter with dead hands and looked about me. A little to the right was a bank of snow, between two prominences.

I sat down on the rug and took off my shoes and rubbed my feet for about five minutes until the I felt the rewarding agony of restored circulation. I put my shoes back on and stood up, opening the rug and wrapping it around me as tightly as possible. Then I bent at the knees until I was almost crouching and threw myself sideways to the ground, and the snowbank closed over me.

I lay there thinking, and when a while had passed I began to weep for Vivian Remington. After a long, long time I finally cried myself into sleep.

# 24

My watch said five minutes after two.

I wasn't thinking straight anymore; something had gone wrong with my reflexes. I turned the corner into Mornington Drive and my dead feet made me feel like I was walking on four inch platforms. A blanket of fat wet snowflakes was descending on the city, curtaining the street lamps so that great patches of white-covered night lay between them, making the street longer, more desolate. I walked from one darkness to another, wondering if everything was as deserted as it looked, afraid at the orbit of every lamp that I was presenting a target to some keen-eyed, trigger-happy cop.

I remember reading once, in a book written by a guy who never left his armchair, that sleeping in the snow makes you warm. He was a liar. It doesn't allow any heat to escape but neither does it give you any. I'd spent seven hours in that snowbank and got out just as cold as I went in. And wetter. I'd have abandoned my clothes if it hadn't made me conspicuous.

My shoes were squelching. My flesh was not merely cold;

it was numb, mortified, finished. I reached into my jacket to check the gun and found my fingers wouldn't open or close. I slipped into a garden and huddled in the evergreens, squatting down and going to work on my hands. I realised suddenly that my lips were drawn back baring my teeth. My chest was heaving rapidly, expelling the breath in shudders. I was dehumanized—an animal. I put the fingers of my right hand into my mouth and they were like sausages.

After a while I dragged myself up again and judged the distance. The Remington house was about a hundred yards away. I crawled over the snow to see if I could make it through the intervening gardens, and the way was barred by an impenetrable hedgerow of privet. I sidled back onto the road, hugging the shadows. The entrance of the Remington driveway yawned like the mouth of a beast through the curtain of falling whiteness.

I could hold the gun now. I took it into my nerveless right hand and tried to creep forward on the toes of my sighing, sucking shoes. In the stillness of the night the noise they made was appalling. I waited until I was between street lights and stopped and eased my shoes off, each with the toe of the other foot. If I was guessing wrong, I wouldn't need shoes again where I was going. If I was guessing right, I'd treat myself to a new pair. I ducked swiftly into the driveway and stopped to get my bearings.

A voice said, "Hey," not very loud, and from two feet away the beam of a flashlight hit me right in the face.

I acted on pure instinct. I lashed out with my gun-weighted right hand, and the bones right up to my shoulder wrenched with pain as I contacted something solid. The light went out abruptly. The red whorls were spinning before my eyes, and I waited for the blast that would fill my belly with lead. I waited five hundred years and nothing happened. I shook my head and looked down with clearing vision. I dropped onto one knee. A young cop of about twenty-three was stretched full length on the snow, black on white, out to the world.

He looked healthy. I didn't know how long he'd stay out and I couldn't afford to take a chance. I crawled on my hands and knees and got one of the large stones that lined the driveway. I put one arm around the cop's shoulders and hefted him to a sitting position and took off his cap. I dropped the stone into it, changed hands, and put the gun into my side pocket. I grabbed the cop by his hair, bent him forward, and picked up the improvised blackjack. The force was hard to judge but I did what I could because he looked like a reasonably good guy. I hit him in the back of the neck and laid him on the snow. Some crazy impulse prompted me to replace his hat before I continued on up to the house.

The garage was closed. Lights were shining from two of the side windows on the second floor and from another up on the third. There appeared to be no more cops outside and I had to take my chance on there being any still in the house. I'd waited this long to make them think I wasn't coming back, to make them believe that maybe I'd got out of town. I hoped they'd been as stupid as that, and the guy in the garden the only guard. My heart was thudding like a tomtom. I sounded like an exhausted dog.

The back of the house was dark, the storm door and the inner door both unlocked. It might be a trap, but I didn't care anymore. Dying wouldn't be so bad. I eased inside and closed the door quietly behind me.

An indescribable bliss of warmth folded round my frozen body. I stood motionless for fully five minutes, luxuriating in it, a sense of relaxation engulfing me in a deep, drowsy lassitude. I had to use an almost physical power of will to prevent myself from curling into a corner and going to sleep.

The dim outline of a chair showed against the window. I sat down on it and peeled off my wet socks. I sat there for another five minutes, trying not to scream as the circulation fought its agonised way back into my frozen feet. I thought of Mrs. Vivian Remington.

I went out into the hall, over the thick gray carpet, and up the stairs, the house silent as the grave. I didn't bother to go to the top story, to Geraldine Astley's room. I remembered the little bitch saying she'd get even with me for turning her down, but that didn't interest me. The motive wasn't strong enough. She was only the smallest of side issues in this case.

On the first landing the two cracks of lights shone out from adjoining rooms. I went noiselessly on the balls of my bare feet and listened at the first door and there was no sound. I shifted the gun to my left hand, quickly turned the handle, stepped inside and closed the door in a single movement. She was sitting up in bed, reading a book and munching candy from the box that lay open beside her. She was looking extremely pretty.

I said: "Were you expecting me, Marian?"

She dropped the book and her hands came up in an involuntary gesture. She stared at me a long time with softening eyes, her head going a little on one side, pitying. "Oh, Mike," she whispered. "Oh, Mike, I'm glad they haven't got you. I've been lying here sick with worry. I couldn't sleep. You're in terrible trouble, Mike. What are you going to do?"

"I don't feel so good," I said. I walked across to the bed and pulled the covers from her. Then I drew back my hand a long way and fetched it hard across her pretty face. She went down onto the pillow and I yanked her up by the hair and hit her again. "Not too much noise," I said. "It looks like Daddy's awake in the next room and I want to talk to you first. Just a few questions and a few answers."

"Your feet are bleeding," she said gently.

I hit her again.

Her eyes went like slits. Her teeth were showing. "You

scum," she snarled, "you filthy low common scum. Where do you think this going to get you? The whole city is hunting you. You're going to hang."

"I know it," I said. "I look forward to it. But I want to go to eternity with nothing puzzling me, everything answered. So—question one: why did you have me watch your stepmother?" I lifted my hand again.

"You like hitting women, don't you?" she sneered.

"Only you. And don't think it won't be harder this time. I'm prepared to fix your face so you shudder every time you get near a mirror. Come on, give. I know some of the answers, but I want to hear them all from your own dear lips."

I guess I looked like I meant it. She lost some of her poise. "I told you, she had a lover. She was dragging my father's name—"

"Cut it! She figured your father was the whole pumpkin patch. She wouldn't look at another guy."

"You saw her yourself, down at the Romilly Club."

"Sure, when she was trying to rescue little hotpants Geraldine from the crummy circle where brother Gerald had introduced her. That was the night she accidentally saved my life. They didn't dare touch me while she was there. She'd have wanted to know what was going on. Which proved to me the she didn't know already."

I felt myself going light-headed. I said: "You wouldn't have cared, would you? In fact, you wanted it; you were in on it. But your stepmother was an innocent, impartial witness; otherwise I'd have been dragged through that door and knocked off before anyone could say knife. I sympathize with you. Nobody expected her to appear that night, and it completely loused up your plans."

"It was you who took me to the Romilly," Marian Remington said levelly.

"Sure, I was more than helpful. Everything was helpful except your stepmother turning up. It must have made you mad when you'd worked so hard to arrange it. I remember you got a little incautious after that, you worked a little too hard to get me to go back to the Romilly. We were going to wait until you were sure your stepmother had gone, and then I could have been knocked off in comfort. Only I wouldn't bite. So you suggested a drive out into the country, along with that corny gag about phoning home first to tell them you'd be late. Who were you going to phone, honey? Your father was supposed to be in New York, your stepmother and sister were at the Romilly, and Gerald was missing. It would have been a swell drive, you'd have enjoyed it. A quiet spot, a little necking, and then whatever guy you'd phoned creeping up behind me and blowing the top off my head."

"You're raving," she said. "You're insane."

"No, just dumb. I should have known that watching your stepmother was only a blind to keep me in hand until I could be put out of the way with the least bother. It was absolutely necessary that I be gotten rid of, wasn't it? You weren't sure how much Gerald had told me before he was knocked off. And when the grapevine told you that his pal Phillip Hughes was in touch with me, you had to have him killed, too. I guess these things get out of hand in your line of business."

"I'm going to scream now," she said quietly.

"Do that and I'll blow your guts out."

Her expression altered almost imperceptibly and I thought she'd changed her mind. I was still dopy with cold, and I didn't know what a little sharpeyes she was. I flashed a glance at the door and it looked shut. She suddenly gave a little moaning cry, did a sort of rolling slump and hit the floor on the far side of the bed. I reached over at her, moving quick, but Remington was quicker. The gun jabbed into my back with a force that almost broke my spine.

"Drop it," he said.

I let the gun fall onto the bed. Marian stood up, straightening her pyjamas, smiling merrily. "I saw the door handle move, Daddy," she said.

"You're a clever girl." His voice sounded dead. He backed away and the pressure went off my spine. I turned around and got a look at him.

He stood tall and straight, dressed in a rich flowered dressing-gown. He looked like a corpse, pained yellow, his eyes blurred blobs of unutterable misery, his face haggard and wretched. He was looking at me with an expression deeper than hatred, sending me all the way to Hell.

And he was holding the gun wrongly. They spend a long time in the Royal Canadian Mounted Police teaching recruits how to take guns away from people who hold them like that. If he didn't pull the trigger right away, all I needed was the opportunity. I moved a step and he backed a step.

I said: "You're a fast worker."

His eyes didn't move. His tongue came out and moistened his lips. His voice was a rattling in his throat. "You murdered my wife," he said.

"Why?" I asked.

The skin tightened all over his head. His teeth showed like fangs. "You murdered my wife," he repeated.

I jabbed a thumb at his daughter and snapped, "Ask her."

His eyes flicked and she wasn't quick enough. The expression came and went like a flash, but he'd seen it. I guess he understood his daughter pretty well: I guess he'd always known the jealous hatred she had for his second wife. He stood staring and then he said, "No," and his head was shaking slowly from side to side. He was off balance and I snapped into action and knocked the gun to the floor, snatching it up and levelling it at him. He took not the slightest notice of me. He just went on staring.

I had spent a long time out in the cold. Tom spent longer and died of it. I'm not a forgiving nor a forgetting type, and someone had to pay for it. I picked my own gun from the bed and leaned against the wall, keeping them covered, watching them, filled with a deep glowing pleasure that warmed me like fire.

She broke when he started to move toward her. She backed into a corner and huddled there, whimpering, "No Daddy, I did it for you, Daddy. She asked him over to talk to him. She was going to tell him. I heard her on the phone."

Her voice died on a whimper, her eyes saucer round, the pupils contracted to pinpoints of fear. She tried to push herself back into the resisting wall, her lips mouthing soundless words. I had never seen anyone so frightened. I did nothing.

He lifted his elegant hands slowly in the air, like a pianist about to strike the fist chord of a concerto. His fingertips came to rest under her eyes, his thumbs levered on her jawbone. Then he clenched and twisted and the fingernails went in and the blood began to flow. He went berserk.

When I tried to drag him off he had her by the back of the neck and was beating her face against the wall. Through her mashed lips she was saying, "Daddy, Daddy," over and over and over. I tapped him behind the ear and he went limp, and I dragged him over and flopped him into a chair. Marian Remington had sunk down in the corner and was making little moans that no longer sounded human. I got the sheets from the bed and tied Remington tight to the chair and gagged him with one of the silken pillow slips. Then I picked up the girl and put her on the bed and wiped her bloody face with the other pillow slip and some water from a pitcher that stood on a little table in the corner.

Her nose looked as if it was broken, and half of one of her front teeth was missing. She didn't look as pretty as she had five minutes before, and I almost felt sorry for her. I splashed what was left of the water into her face, and suddenly she sat up and put her feet on the floor. I said:

"Nice Daddy. But I guess you need to be a pretty tough egg when you're top boy in the Syndicate."

"He didn't know what he was doing," she said tonelessly. "He never hit me before, not even when I was a child. It was that woman made him do it, that unspeakable whore of a woman."

My sympathy for her went down the drain. I said: "You rotten little bitch, be satisfied with you killed her and stop running her into the ground. He was in love with her, but you wouldn't know about that. Start telling me about some of the things you do know."

She looked up at me, and even now she was attempting a sneering grin. "This only makes your case so much worse," she said. "Go to hell."

"You force me to take steps."

"Such as?"

"Such as filling your father's belly with bullets. I've nothing to lose."

It didn't faze her. "You're not the type," she said.

Remington's eyes were open. He was regarding us over the top of the gag with an expressionless gaze. The girl made a move toward him. I pushed her back and waved the gun. She said: "I'm sorry, Daddy, but you'll realise in the end that I had to do it. I didn't mind your hitting me. I forgive you. Please forgive me, too. I had to do it."

"Sit back and listen," I told her, "and correct me when I'm wrong. We'll start right at the beginning."

"I said for you to go to hell."

"I've been," I said, "and come back. We'll commence with the night Mrs. Remington asked me to come here. She was worried about Gerald. He was leading a wild life and spending too much money, and she wondered where it was all coming from. She didn't know he was blackmailing his stepfather because he'd discovered Daddy was head of the Quebec Syndicate. Right so far?"

"Go to hell."

"Your repartee is monotonous," I said. "We get nowhere.

I didn't want to do this, but you leave me no choice."

I picked up a large metal ashtray that stood beside the bed. I went over to Remington and took the ashtray by its rim and judged my distance. "Okay?" I asked.

She made no answer.

"Don't move or cry out, or I'll kill him." I swung the ashtray and hit Remington hard on the side of his kneecap. A muffled scream came from behind the gag, and the sweat broke out on his forehead. I remembered how I'd felt one day playing football without pads, and I was glad it was him and not me. "He's got one more knee, two elbows, and other interesting joints," I said. "He'll find it painful. He'll maybe not walk again."

She had gone rigid. The blood drained from her face, leaving the bruises stark. "What do you want to know?" she whispered, watching her father writhe against his bonds. "Don't hit him again."

"How did Gerald discover Daddy was boss of the Syndicate?"

She slumped down beaten, submissive. "It was Gerald's friend Phillip Hughes. He started taking cocaine and Gerald found out. They went to a party or something and somebody gave Gerald a message to bring home to Daddy. They thought it was all right because Gerald was his stepson."

"So Gerald started blackmailing," I said, "and jacked up the weekly fee as his tastes got more expensive. And when Daddy called a halt to rising prices, Gerald threatened to go to the police. Or even a private detective. That's where I came in. Or was it?"

"My stepmother had no idea what was going on," the girl said, "and Daddy and I thought that Gerald might have had something to do with calling you in, especially after he went out with you that night. We knew you weren't a decorator; Daddy went upstairs and checked you over the phone. We thought Gerald might be bluffing."

"But you couldn't take a chance, eh? And anyway he'd got out of hand. So you had him knocked off. And for safety's sake you thought you'd better knock me off as well, only you first had to find out whether I knew anything and whether I'd told anybody else. That didn't work so you knocked me off anyway, only a mistake was made and a Mountie was killed instead. Funny coincidence. He was a narcotics man. In a little while he'd have been on to that sideline your father goes in for."

She shrugged.

"Question," I said. "How did your father persuade Mrs. Remington to give me the boot?"

Marian Remington actually smiled. "Daddy told her some of his imports had come through without duty being paid on them. He said you might find out and report to the Revenue people and there would be a scandal. My stepmother was a rather stupid woman. Anything else you'd like to know?"

"Why did Charlie Hedges come here on the night Gerald disappeared. Just to report that he was dead?"

"In a way that was a mistake," she said, "although it was really safer than the telephone. The little man was under the influence of drugs and he wanted to boast. Daddy handled him all right."

"Daddy's pretty smart," I said, "except when he refuses to identify bodies in morgues."

She was still smiling. She said almost gaily, "We have a plan. We're going to pin Gerald's murder on you."

"Daddy's little right hand girl. What's an extra murder to me? Even your father's?"

She went sober again. "You won't get away with this."

"I don't want to. I'm just satisfying my vulgar curiosity. Where does Geraldine fit into the pattern?"

"Nowhere. She followed Gerald to the Romilly one night and liked what she saw. She's too stupid to think of anything but men. She's like her mother."

"I guess she's lucky you didn't murder her, too," I said. "I'll congratulate her when I see her. Anything else I ought to know?"

"What good will it do you?"

I went over to Remington and took off his gag. I said: "What other distribution centers do you use for narcotics beside the Romilly and the barbotte joint? And what are your other connections besides gambling?"

He was smooth. "I am willing to tell you the story of my life from the day I was born," he said. "It will prove of not the slightest use to you. I am well covered, and I shall naturally deny everything you tell the police"—he smiled—"that is if you can get near the police without being shot on sight. And if you force one or both of us to sign a confession, a shall refute that, too. My daughter's face and my own knee will be proof that it was obtained under duress."

"I'm sorry for what I did," the girl said. "Truly sorry, Daddy. I thought I was doing it for the best."

"We'll not talk about that," he said to her. "For the present we'll confine ourselves to putting Mr. Garfin as they say, on toast."

All at once he began to laugh, a polite cultured sound that made me think, although it was totally different of the way the bloodwagon guys had laughed when they carted away Tom's frozen body. I guess Remington had cause to laugh. It must have seemed very funny to him. The fire under the toast got hotter, and I went crazy. I clouted him across the face, but his mirth only got louder. The girl must have seen the humor of it for suddenly she began to laugh too, a giggle that grew and grew and grew. I couldn't take it. My face blazed hot and my ears were pounding, and when I looked at Remington he seemed to be tinged with red. I lifted the gun and put the snout between his eyes.

"I'm going to kill you, Remington," I said.

The effects of cold or temper or both had made me

careless. Remington had not properly closed the door when he came in. I didn't hear anything but the laughter and the pounding in my ears. And then a voice said: "I wouldn't do that if I were you, Garfin."

My finger was tightening on the trigger. I could still have shot him, even if a bullet ripped into my back. But I guess they were right. I'm not the type.

"Don't do it," the voice said, "it's not worth it."

I dropped the gun onto Remington's knees, hoping it would go off of its own accord. Then I turned around and looked into the eye of the gun in Frankisson's hand. He was standing in the doorway, flanked on one side by a large cop, and on the other by Geraldine Astley. The beaver-faced maid was in back, peering over his shoulder.

"Thank God you've come, Mr. Frankisson," Remington said wearily. "We've been having rather a bad time."

Frankisson smiled bleakly. "Yes, I know. I've been standing outside the door for the past few minutes. You Remingtons have penetrating voices."

"What was he doing when you gave that yell?" Geraldine Astley asked maliciously. She undulated into the room and stood in front of her stepsister, hands on her hips. "My God, your face!" she said joyfully. "You look awful."

Frankisson motioned the cop. "Get the others from downstairs and call the wagon to take these two away." The cop moved to the bannister and began to shout and Frankisson turned to Marian Remington. "Better get your clothes on," he said. "You're going on a trip, and I don't think you'll be back."

The sound of copper feet came bashing up the stairs. I sank down onto the bed, and I was trembling. Frankisson regarded me with an expression that was the nearest thing to curiosity he's ever worn. "You had it pretty close there for a while, Garfin," he said. "You'd make a good policeman. I like your methods."

It sounded as if he were admiring me.

# 25

I sprawled in one of the Remington armchairs and downed my second tumbler of Scotch, only half listening to what Frankisson had to say.

"I left word that any one of them was to call me personally," he continued, "the moment they saw or heard anything suspicious. So a little while ago, the girl, what's-her-name, Geraldine, went outside to see the cop on guard, Fortier. She wanted to offer him a cup of cocoa, she says, and I doubt it, but it doesn't matter. She found him sprawled in the bushes, out cold."

"She'd take anything to bed," I said, "even a cop named Fortier. All the same, I owe him an apology."

Frankisson drew on his cigarette and blew the smoke in twin streams from his nose. "A cop named Fortier is going to be on the mat for neglect of duty. And incidentally, a guy named Garfin is going to be charged with assaulting a cop named Fortier."

"Witnesses?" I asked.

"Then maybe not." He must have liked the smoke through the nostrils routine. He did it again. It looked phony on him. "You were lucky," he said, "that I had sense enough to wait outside that door." He nodded at me. "I approve of your methods. You'd make a good cop."

"Some other time. Can I go home now?"

He shook his head. "A few more questions. And half the force is still looking for you, so you'd be shot on sight."

"You'd care."

"Not a bit. You're a credit to yourself and an ornament to your profession, but I don't like you very much."

"Lover," I said.

I went into the hall and thumbed the phone book, and found Collis's private number. I must have awakened him.

He sounded thick. I said: "You'll be making a few dope raids tonight. Frankisson will tell you about it when he gets good and ready. The credit belongs to Tom Littlejohn. They're the guys who killed him. Treat 'em rough."

"Yes," he said. "Thank you, Garfin." And that wall he said, but it made me feel awful good.

I dialled a second number. It was answered on the first ring so I guess the Lindsay was reading the ghost stories in her sitting room. "Mike," I told her. "Everything's all right. Go to bed."

"The police have been here," she said. "I think they're still out in the street. You're in trouble."

"Not anymore."

"I'm sure you are. You always are. Come home and tell me about it."

"I don't want to tell anybody anything," I said. "Go to bed. I'll not be home tonight. See you in the morning." I hung up with the feeling that I'd been let down.

I was dialling the third number when Geraldine's busy hands began to wander. "Beat it," I told her, but she took no notice. I gave her a shove that sent her to the other side of the hall. "Go look for your cop," I said, "the dwarf won't be there any more." I could hear Tessie's voice batting in my ear.

"The cops are still here," she said.

"Tell them to go home, the party's over. Everything's fine. Tess."

"You bum! You give me more worry—"

Geraldine Astley was back, trying to sit on my lap. I cracked her across the wrist and nearly did myself a permanent injury. "I told you to beat it," I said.

Tessie's voice went sharp. "You've got a woman there."

"I sure have."

"You crumb," she said angrily, "can't you ever get it off your mind. Here I sit sweating hour after hour and all the time—"

"Goodnight," I said, and hung up.

I took Geraldine Astley under the arms and carried her across the hall. She was more than willing. I put her in the clothes closet and shut the door on her and rammed a chair under the handle. I went back to the phone. She started beating on the door and yelling to be let out. I called the station and asked for Masson and my credit was good. They put me through immediately.

"Is that nice fat wife of yours asleep?" I asked.

"At this time of night? Sure."

"Call her. Remind her she once invited me for a meal. Tell her to get up and cook it now, a big meal. I'm hungry."

He thought a while. "Okay," he said.

"I'll be down at the station in a little while. We'll go to your home."

He said: "I'm glad it worked out the way it did, Michel."

"So am I," I said. "See you."

I went back into the other room and picked up Frankisson. I was wearing a pair of shoes I'd taken from Remington's wardrobe and they were pinching my feet.

"Ready?" Frankisson asked.

"Yes," I said testily.

We went down the snowy drive toward the waiting police car. Back in the house Geraldine Astley was still hammering the door, yelling to be let out.

All down the street I could hear the drip, drip, drip, of falling water. The thaw had started.

**THE END**

www.vehiculepress.com